Mark Golding

With Illustrations by Lucian Gradinariu

Out of Time

 Bumblebee
Books

A CIP catalogue record for this title is
available from the British Library.

ISBN: 978-1-83934-758-0

First Published in 2023

Bumblebee Books
Tallis House
2 Tallis Street
London
EC4Y 0AB

Printed in Great Britain

Dedication

This book is dedicated to a wonderful Mum and Dad
who always encouraged me to follow my dreams.
I miss you both and think about you everyday.
I hope that I've made you proud.

Part 1: Max

Chapter 1

Sunday 9th January 2022

Bang!

The blast had been sufficient to knock 12-year-old Joe Jackson to the floor, with enough force to render him unconscious.

As the dust began to settle, the ground around the site of the explosion weakened to such an extent that a large hole began to form – unfortunately, the ground started giving way at the exact spot where Joe was lying.

The small town of Highcross was a typical community located in the middle of England. It had a relatively small population and included the type of boring high street that can be found in many places throughout the country. It's a quiet, sleepy kind of town. The type of town in which very little happens.

There was, however, one interesting fact about Highcross: during the Second World War, it was home to a very important munitions factory. This had obviously made it a target for the Luftwaffe[1] , and it also explained why there had just been an enormous explosion. It was quite common for unexploded World War II bombs to be found in Highcross, and that's exactly what had just happened on this wintery Sunday afternoon.

"Great job!" shouted the supervisor of the bomb disposal team who had just dealt superbly with the latest unexploded bomb.

1. The German Airforce during WWII

None of the team had seen Joe exploring the area and so were completely unaware that he'd fallen through the ground just a few metres from where they were currently standing.

"Let's get packed away, lads!" shouted the supervisor. "Just cordon off that hole. We'll get it filled tomorrow," he added, before leaving the scene with the rest of his team.

A few minutes later, Joe started to come round. *Where am I?* he thought hazily, lifting his head and glancing around him.

Joe was a little more curious and adventurous than the typical Highcross youngster. He was of average height for a boy of his age, with slightly messy ginger hair and two distinctive moles on the left side of his face. He wasn't remotely interested in the usual things 12-year-old boys are generally so passionate about, such as football. Instead, Joe had a flair for travel and adventure, often finding himself in tricky situations. In the last year alone, two search parties had been launched because Joe had managed to get himself lost. He had never, however, found himself underground before.

Why did I try to find an unexploded bomb? he wondered. *I'm such an idiot! How am I supposed to get out of here?!*

Suddenly, Joe remembered that he had his mobile phone on him. He pulled it out of his pocket and, to his complete surprise, found it undamaged. There was, however, no signal.

"Help!" he shouted, as loud as he could.

There was no response.

He was on the very outskirts of town, and it was rare for people to come here, though he supposed there might be the occasional dog walker.

Of course, unbeknown to Joe, the area had been cordoned off.

"Help!" he shouted for a second time.

Once again, there was no response.

How long have I been unconscious for? he wondered.

He was starting to get very worried now. After all, the hole was far too deep for him to climb out of. However, when he turned on the flashlight on his phone, he saw something interesting – something that gave him hope.

This wasn't just a hole. There was a passage leading off it.

Maybe this will lead to an exit! he thought excitedly as he headed into the dark passage. Most people would have been scared to walk down a dark, underground passage alone, but not Joe. To him, this was just another adventure.

Joe made his way along the passage for five minutes, with only his mobile phone flashlight illuminating the way. Then, slowly but surely, the passage opened out into what appeared to be a large cave. Slowly, Joe flashed his torch around the space – it was enormous.

After checking his phone battery, which had plenty of charge left, he walked further into the cave and waved the flashlight around again.

Out of the corner of his eye, he saw something flicker.

What was that? he thought, spinning around.

He was getting scared now. He was sure something had moved in the cave.

He stood still for a few moments, listening intently, and what he heard made his blood run cold. Footsteps seemed to be approaching him from behind.

He swung around in the direction of the sound and shone the flashlight in front of him. Joe wasn't the type of person to feel fear; that's why he was so accustomed to getting into scrapes. Right now, however, he was terrified.

There was somebody in the cave with him.

***

Mrs Jackson was frantic. She knew that Joe often found himself in difficult situations, and she was used to him coming home at different times, but he wasn't normally this late.

"He'll be okay, Patricia," said Mrs Jackson's next-door neighbour, Eve. "He always turns up."

This didn't help Mrs Jackson feel any better. It also didn't help that Mr Jackson worked on an oil rig in the North Sea for half the year; this certainly made dealing with Joe's 'adventures' even more challenging.

"We need to go and look for him," said a tearful Mrs Jackson. "No one has any idea where he went after this afternoon!"

"Of course," said Eve. "I've already asked our neighbours; they're looking for him now. We'll find him, don't worry."

***

A couple of miles away, the search party had already started looking for Joe in an area of Highcross where he'd gone missing before. Of course, they didn't realise that Joe was on the other side of town.

"Joe!" came the shouts of the crowd. It was very dark now and the temperature was dropping rapidly.

"It's much too cold for anyone to survive out here overnight," said one of the worried members of the search party.

"Don't be so negative," said another.

After a while, Mrs Jackson and Eve joined the search party. They had decided not to tell Mr Jackson. *There's no need to worry him yet*, thought Eve. *We'll find him soon.*

After an unsuccessful hour, however, the group was ready to abandon the search.

"It's too dark to see anything," said one of the searchers, "we have to call the police."

It was at this moment that another member of the group remembered something. "There was an unexploded bomb disposal over by the railway bridge earlier today," he told Joe's mum.

Mrs Jackson took a deep breath, trying not to panic.

"Don't worry," Eve told her in a soothing tone, trying to keep her calm. "He won't be there; the bomb disposal unit will have checked for people in the area."

Mrs Jackson nodded, though she didn't look convinced.

"We'll go and have a look!" came a shout from the crowd. "You go home and wait by the phone."

A tired Mrs Jackson agreed, heading back to her house with Eve whilst the rest of the group headed over to the site of the earlier controlled explosion.

"Look at this," said David – one of the members of the search party – as he looked down at the cordoned off hole in the ground, "it's enormous!"

Slowly, the search party inched closer to the hole, peering down into its depths.

"Some of us are going to have to go down there," David continued. "Do we have enough torches?"

"Yes, we do," came a response from the crowd. "We have plenty."

"Okay," said David, turning to the rest of the group, "are there any volunteers willing to come into the hole with me?"

The people of Highcross were always very proud of their role as helpful members of the community, and – as a result – it didn't take long for six people to volunteer.

"Okay," said David, "let's go down and have a look. The rest of you stay here, and if we aren't back within an hour, call the police and the fire brigade."

The others nodded, exchanging apprehensive looks.

With that, the seven brave volunteers made their way, slowly and carefully, into the hole.

"There's a passage here!" David said to the others, once they were all down. "Let's go and have look!"

After making sure everyone had a torch, David led the way into the dark passage that Joe had only recently entered himself.

***

"Who's there?" asked Joe, his voice shaking.

There was no reply.

"I know there's someone there... I just saw you!" he shouted.

"Please leave me alone," said a quiet voice from the darkness. "Just turn back and go."

Joe jumped at the sound of the voice. "Are you trapped down here?" he asked after a moment.

Again, there was no answer.

By now Joe was beginning to feel extremely uneasy. There could be anybody down here with him! "You're making me nervous," he said quietly.

"Don't be nervous," came the reply, "I'm not going to hurt you. I just want to be left alone."

After a moment of hesitation, Joe shone his phone flashlight in the direction of the voice and, finally, he saw who was in the cave with him. "You're just a kid!" he gasped.

"My name is Maxelon," said the stranger, "and I come from the planet Proxima Centauri b."

Joe took a step back. Now he was feeling even more uneasy. *Great,* he thought, *I'm down here with a crazy person.*

Maxelon looked like he was about 15 years old. His skin was very pale, and he had jet black hair. He was wearing a silver suit with what looked like a black waistcoat. Hanging at his waist, he wore a utility belt with lots of strange-looking gadgets hanging from it.

"What are you talking about?" asked Joe, just as the cave lit up. He took another step back, shocked at the sudden illumination.

"You don't need your torch anymore," said Maxelon.

Joe looked around him in awe. The cave was unbelievable, its walls covered in different coloured rocks and what looked like sparkling gemstones. In the centre of the cave stood an amazing-looking computer.

"What is that?" asked Joe, pointing at the machine.

"It's my console," explained Maxelon. "It's for contacting my planet. It should also let me travel between here and there."

Joe looked at Maxelon, frowning. "Should?"

"It's broken," sighed Maxelon. "I've been stuck on this planet for almost a year."

Joe approached the console and looked at the blank monitor. "How did you get here?" he asked.

Maxelon explained that he had accidently crashed here during a visit to our galaxy. "My ship was destroyed on impact, but I was able to grow this computer. I had hoped it would help me get home, but I've not been able to power it up," he said sadly.

"Grow a computer?" asked a very suspicious Joe. He was beginning to think that someone was playing a trick on him. He looked around the cave to see if there were any hidden cameras. He might be on one of those game shows.

"Yes," replied Maxelon. "We can organically grow our technology. We call it *Organa-tech* and, thankfully, I'd brought plenty of seeds with me."

Joe was feeling even more confused when, suddenly, the console came to life. "What's happening?" he asked, wide-eyed.

Maxelon ran over to the monitor. "It must be picking up power from the satellites around the planet," he told Joe. "The hole that just appeared in the ground is letting the signal through! There's not enough power to contact home, but it will allow me to charge my trekker."

"Your trekker?" asked Joe.

Before Maxelon could answer, the sound of voices floated over to them – someone was entering the cave. In an instant the console powered down and the light that had been illuminating the cave went out. Apart from the occasional beam of torchlight, the cave was engulfed in darkness once again.

"There you are!" shouted David, running over to Joe. "Your mum's worried sick!"

"Maxelon?" shouted Joe, looking around the cave.

There was no sign of his new friend and, just like before, there was no response.

"Who are you talking to?" asked a bewildered David.

"Nobody," replied Joe quickly.

David and the other six members of the search party looked around the cave, but there was nobody else there.

David turned back to Joe, concerned. "We need to go."

The group headed carefully down the passage and back to the hole, where they were helped up by the waiting members of the search party. As they walked, the only things Joe could think about were Maxelon and his strange homegrown computer.

Chapter 2

Monday 10th January 2022

"Time to get up, Joseph!"

Joe opened his eyes to see his mum looking down at him.

"You don't want to be late for school."

Joe yawned loudly. He was tired; it had been a late night.

"I'm sorry for shouting at you last night when you got home," said Mrs Jackson, gently placing a hand on her son's arm, "I was just angry. I'd been so worried!"

"I'm sorry, Mum," said Joe quietly. "Are you going to tell Dad?"

Mrs Jackson had already decided she wasn't going to worry her husband while he was so far away. "As long as nothing like this happens again," she told Joe, "then there's no need for your dad to find out."

"Thanks, Mum."

With that, Mrs Jackson left Joe's room and headed downstairs to make breakfast.

"Hi Milo," said Joe as he sat up in bed.

Milo was the family cat who frequently slept at the end of Joe's bed, and Joe considered him to be one of his best friends; they would often sit together while Joe told him tales of his recent adventures.

"You don't judge me, do you?" Joe said to Milo. "You can keep a secret, can't you?" The cat just stared at him. "I think I met an alien yesterday," Joe continued.

Milo looked at him for a couple more seconds before scampering downstairs for his breakfast.

After breakfast, Joe packed up his bag and headed out for the day.

"Have a lovely day at school," said Mrs Jackson, "but make sure you come straight home after."

"I promise," replied Joe.

Joe meant what he said about going home on time; he had absolutely no intention of getting back late. He also, however, had no intention of going to school. He simply had far too many unanswered questions.

Had he imagined what had happened in the cave? Was there really an alien living under Highcross? And what on earth (or not) was a trekker?

I need to find out what's going on down there, he thought as he walked down the street, away from his house.

Joe made his way carefully to the railway bridge, making sure to stay away from the main routes where he might be seen by teachers or classmates.

Before long, he was back at the hole. There was still a rope cordon around it, but it hadn't yet been filled in.

Am I crazy? he thought as he lowered himself down into the hole. Today, it was much easier to see the way, as the bright morning winter sun was illuminating the hole. It also made it much easier to see the passage he'd walked through the evening before.

"Maxelon!" he shouted as he walked along, the light from the sun getting weaker and weaker until, once again, he found himself in pitch blackness.

He reached for his phone, turned the flashlight on, and held it out in front of him as he walked. He could see the entrance to the cave getting closer and closer, and as he entered the cave, it immediately lit up just like it did before.

Maxelon was standing at the console in the centre of the cave.

"Hello again," said Joe, relieved that Maxelon and the computer were still here – relieved that he wasn't going crazy.

"Hello," replied Maxelon, turning to face him. "Why have you come back?"

"I needed to check that this was real," he said, gesturing at the computer and the cave in general.

"Well, it's nice to see you again. It's been very lonely down here," admitted Maxelon.

Nodding, Joe approached the central console. "Is it still working?" he asked.

"Yes," replied Maxelon. "It's not at full power, but I've managed to charge my trekker. I've also been able to charge my Silver Sphere."

"What's a Silver Sphere?" asked Joe.

"I'll show you later."

As Joe walked around the computer, inspecting every part, Maxelon explained that he came from a city called Tamiran. There were two species living on Proxima Centauri b, he said. The Tamirans were a peaceful and technologically rich species who had been trying to find life on other planets to make friends with. The other species on Proxima Centauri b were the Wolfians. They were warmongering creatures who aimed to take over any other planet they could find. However, they didn't have the technology to travel to different worlds like the Tamirans did.

Joe listened to all of this, utterly transfixed; he was fascinated by the story of life on another planet.

"Do you mind if I call you Max?" he asked, once Maxelon had finished.

"Why?" asked Maxelon.

"It sounds better," Joe replied, shrugging. "My full name is Joseph, but I much prefer Joe."

Maxelon thought about this for a second. "Max sounds great," he agreed.

Joe nodded. "Max it is."

Max took what looked like a magnifying glass from his utility belt.

"Why do you have a magnifying glass?" asked Joe, intrigued.

"This is how people from Tamiran travel," Max explained. "It's called a trekker. It can take me anywhere in the world."

Joe couldn't believe what he was hearing. "So you're saying… we could go anywhere in the world? Right now?"

"We?" Max responded.

"Yes," Joe replied. "We. Me and you. I promise I won't say a word about any of this to anyone."

"I need to go to the Pyramids of Egypt," said Max.

Joe could barely contain his excitement. "I've always wanted to see the Great Pyramids!" he exclaimed. "We've literally just studied them in school."

Max pressed a button on the handle of the trekker and an image of the pyramids appeared in the glass.

Then, suddenly, a swirling portal appeared in front of the magnifying glass, which Max simply walked straight through. Though he hesitated a little, Joe thought it would be best to follow.

There was a flash of light as he passed through the portal, and then there was just darkness.

***

"Where are you?" Joe shouted, panicked.

There was no response.

Joe glanced around in the gloom, terrified. It was then that he noticed a light coming towards him.

"Joe, stay there." It was Max. As he got closer, Joe realised he was wearing a torch on his belt.

"Where are we?" Joe asked. "I thought we were going to see the pyramids."

Max looked at Joe. "And that's exactly where we are," he replied.

"I'm confused," said Joe. "It just seems like you've brought us to another cave somewhere."

Max sighed. He was beginning to look frustrated. "Joe, we are at the pyramids," he told him. "The trekker has brought us exactly where we wanted to go. We are inside the Great Pyramid."

"Oh," said Joe, looking around him.

Noticing a ray of light coming from a corridor ahead, they started walking towards it. As they got closer to the sunlight, Joe could feel the excitement growing inside him, getting stronger and stronger. He was inside one of the pyramids!

This must be a dream, he thought.

As they stepped out into the light, however, Joe knew he couldn't possibly be dreaming. The heat of the Egyptian desert hit him in an instant, the brightness of the sun making him squint. He was about to see the pyramids.

The sight was even better than he could have imagined, the outline of the three huge pyramids dominating the skyline as he stared up at the impressive structures.

They spent 20 minutes wandering around the pyramids, Max looking very carefully at all the stones that made up the building blocks.

"What are you looking for?" asked Joe.

"Nothing you need to worry about," replied Max, before stopping in his tracks. "Come on, let's go home."

Joe was disappointed at having to leave ─ after all, this had been the strangest and most unbelievable day of his life – but at the same time he knew he had to get home. Max asked Joe to keep everything he'd seen and heard today a secret, and Joe nodded his understanding.

When Max pulled out the trekker, Joe saw that it was now showing an image of the cave under Highcross. Just as before, a portal appeared, but just as they were about to walk through it, the ground started to shake. A second later, the portal closed.

"What's going on?" Joe asked Max.

The shaking got worse and worse until there was a great flash of light and some kind of sonic boom. Joe and Max were thrown instantly to the floor.

After a few disorientating seconds, Joe opened his eyes and stood up. He could hear people behind him screaming and shouting. They were pointing in the direction of the pyramids.

When he turned around, he realised why the people were so upset – the pyramids were gone!

Max was sitting on the ground, his head in his hands as he mumbled to himself. Joe could just make out the four words he was repeating over and over.

"I was too late."

***

They were simply gone. One minute, Joe and Max had been standing in front of the pyramids, and the next… they were just… gone!

"Where are they?" asked an extremely startled Joe.

"Well," said Max, "it's a rather long story." He went on to explain that the pyramids had been stolen by a thief from Proxima Centauri b and transported far back in time. The thief's name was Dardan and he was the leader of the Wolfians. He had stowed away on Max's spacecraft so he could travel to Earth, and he'd tried to take control of the ship. This was what had caused it to crash to Earth.

The crash – and subsequent explosion – of Max's ship had been so powerful that it had opened a portal into time. Max had been stranded in the 21st century, while Dardan had been thrown much further back in time. Unfortunately, he had access to the same technology as Max.

"He was able to steal some *Organa-tech* seeds," explained Max, "so he's been able to grow a computer just like mine. The pyramids are very powerful; they're full of ancient mystical power. Clearly, Dardan has been able to power up enough energy to transport them back to the past." He sighed. "I'm not sure where his source of power has come from, but the pyramids will provide him with unlimited energy, so he'll be able to travel wherever and whenever he wants to. And, more importantly, he'll be able to transport other Wolfians to this planet."

Joe frowned. "Wait... you said travel wherever and whenever? Does he have a time machine?"

"Yes, he does," replied Max casually.

"Let's go then!" Joe shouted, getting very excited now. This was shaping up to be his most amazing adventure yet! "We need to stop him!" he added.

Max gave Joe a disapproving look. "I can't take you with me; this isn't a game. It's extremely dangerous. I shouldn't have even brought you here – I'm taking you home."

Joe, however, wasn't going to take no for an answer. "You can't go alone," he pointed out, "you've already said it will be very dangerous."

Max shook his head. "I'm sorry but it's just too risky. You have a family you need to get back to. It's time for you to go home." Once again, Max raised the trekker out in front him. He was careful to check that nobody could see what he was doing, but everyone was more concerned with the missing pyramids anyway.

Once again, the image of the cave appeared in the magnifying glass and a portal appeared in front of them. Quickly, Joe and Max walked through the swirling portal, soon finding themselves back in the cave.

"What's so special about the pyramids?" asked Joe once the portal had disappeared.

"What do you mean?" responded Max.

"You told me that they were very powerful. What were you looking for there?" Joe asked.

Max leant against the central console. "You are the first person from Earth to learn the truth about some of the ancient monuments," he explained.

Joe gave Max his full attention, listening intently to every word he was saying.

"This planet has been visited many times by life from other galaxies," Max began. "Dardan and I are not the first. The ancient people of Earth had friendly alliances with many different extra-terrestrial visitors. As tokens of friendship, these visitors often left gifts for the people of Earth. Many of your ancient monuments – such as the pyramids and Stonehenge – are extra-terrestrial. They still contain the power of these ancient aliens."

Joe shook his head in wonder. He was simply amazed at this story. "What happened to all these aliens?" he asked.

Max shrugged. "Nobody knows. They were ancient alien races, so they might have gone extinct. Proxima Centauri b was also visited by them, but approximately 4,500 Earth years ago, the visits stopped. Us Tamirans continue to celebrate the visitors, whereas – for some unknown reason – the people of Earth forgot."

"This is amazing!" said Joe. "So tell me: what were you looking for at the pyramids?"

Max explained that he was checking for movement. "When my console powered up yesterday, I was able to find out exactly when but not where Dardan is. I could also see that a strange signal had been building over the centre of Cairo. I knew it must be Dardan trying to use the power of the pyramids. I was hoping I'd have enough time to time-lock the pyramids, but I needed to wait for my console to gain more power."

Joe had become so captivated by this amazing story that he'd totally forgotten to check the time. When he glanced down at his watch, he gasped. "Oh no, school finished an hour ago – I need to get home! Are you still going to be here tomorrow?"

Max approached the keyboard on the central console. "I'm afraid not. I need to stop Dardan from doing too much damage and make sure I can take him back to Proxima Centauri b. It has been really nice meeting you, Joe. Thank you for being so friendly."

Feeling rather sad, Joe said goodbye and turned to walk back down the passage. As he did so, the cave started vibrating and the roof started to collapse. "What's happening?!" he screamed.

Max had no idea; he could only watch helplessly as the entrance to the passage was completely blocked by falling rocks.

"I'm trapped!" shouted Joe.

***

The central console was now lit up like a Christmas tree. Max was frantically pressing all kinds of buttons, but nothing seemed to be working.

"What's happening?" shouted Joe.

Max had absolutely no idea, but he knew it had to be Dardan who was causing it.

The monitor powered up and a series of numbers and images flashed on and off the screen. "So that's where he is," Max said to himself as, once again, the monitor went blank.

Suddenly, the console started beeping. "We need to go," said Max, "now."

"Where?" asked Joe.

"Anywhere. The console is going to explode!" said Max as he grabbed the trekker from his belt. He pressed the button on the side of the strange magnifying glass and an image appeared on the glass. This was followed by another swirling portal.

"Run!" ordered Max.

They both ran through the portal and found themselves standing on the bank of the River Thames in Central London.

"We're in London!" Joe exclaimed. "This is so weird!"

"My cave and console have been destroyed," Max sighed. "Unless I can find Dardan, I'm going to be trapped here forever."

Sitting down, Joe and Max looked out over the river towards the Houses of Parliament.

"If Dardan gets his way, this will be destroyed as well. I need to find him," said Max.

All this talk of destruction was scaring Joe; his sense of adventure had been severely challenged today. He had a feeling, however, that Max couldn't capture Dardan on his own. "Can you also travel in time?" he asked.

"Yes," said Max.

Joe thought for a moment. "Does that mean that you could go to wherever Dardan is, capture him, and return back to this exact time?"

"Yes," replied Max.

"So… are you going to travel through time to find Dardan?"

"Yes," said Max again.

"Can I come with you?" Joe asked.

Max thought about this for a second as he looked at all the people enjoying their peaceful lives in the wonderful City of London. "Yes," replied Max. "I need your help."

Part 2: The Cretaceous Period

Chapter 3

Max had finally admitted that he needed Joe's help and had agreed that they'd be going on a journey together to find Dardan. "I think I know where the pyramids have been taken," he said.

Joe asked him whether they were going to go back in time straightaway.

Max said yes but that Joe needed some training first. "Before we go after Dardan, you'll have to go on a short trip back to the year 1999," he informed him. "This will ensure that your body can cope with travelling through time before we go even further back."

"Where is your time machine?" asked Joe, thinking about the destruction of the cave.

Max pulled out a small ball from his pocket as he replied, "Let's go somewhere quieter."

After finding a quiet alley, Max threw the ball on the ground. There was a loud bang and, suddenly, a large silver ball appeared in front of them, the same size as a small car.

"This is the Silver Sphere," said Max, opening a door in the side of the ball, "climb in."

Inside, there were two seats and a console with lots of buttons.

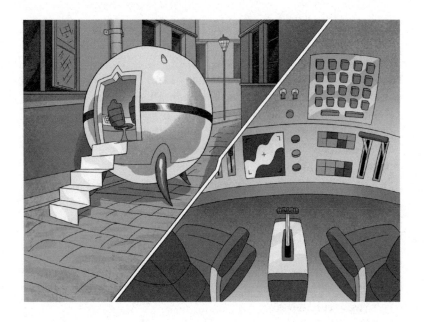

Max typed in the date of their destination – 31st December 1999 – and a time of 11.57pm. Then, as the door of the sphere began to close, a timer appeared in front of Joe. It was counting backwards from the year 2022.

While the numbers counted down, Joe watched the monitor in front of him. He could see famous world events being shown on the screen, but they were all going in reverse. As the sphere started spinning, Joe began to feel dizzy, and – as the timer counted down to 1999 – he started feeling like he was going to be sick.

Fortunately, he wasn't sick, and after a short while they stopped spinning and the door slid open.

"We're here!" announced Max.

As they stepped out of the time machine and onto the London street, Max explained to Joe that he'd feel better in a minute or two. It was just the shock of his first time travel journey.

Before long, Joe heard a loud voice counting down from ten over some kind of big speaker. The crowd that was gathered at the side of the River Thames started to count down as well.

"Ten, nine, eight, seven, six, five, four, three, two, one!" the crowd chanted in unison until Joe heard the following from the announcer: "Welcome to the year 2000!"

Joe couldn't believe he was actually here. He had travelled back in time! His mum and dad had told him all about the millennium celebrations, but he never imagined he'd get to experience it for himself. He took a moment to just breathe in the excitable atmosphere.

"Well done," said Max. "You are officially a time traveller, but now we have a long journey ahead of us."

The two of them got back into the Silver Sphere and Max typed in a date. The door glided to a close, the sphere started to spin, and the countdown began once again. Max explained that they were going to return to Highcross before travelling back to the Cretaceous period.

Joe had to check what Max had just said. "The Cretaceous period?"

"Yes," replied Max.

"The dinosaur times?" asked Joe.

"Yes," said Max.

***

Joe felt dizzy as he stepped out of the time machine, but that soon passed when he looked around at their new surroundings – he simply could not believe what he was seeing! Stretching out in front of him was a landscape the kind of which he'd only ever seen in films or read about in books.

They were in a forest clearing, with a small lake directly in front of them and a large volcano further in the distance. The volcano had smoke coming out of it, billowing into the sky in huge swirling spirals. The temperature was extremely warm and tropical – a far cry from the London they'd just come from.

"Are we still in England?" asked Joe, stretching his arms high into the sky and enjoying the heat.

"We are on the land that will eventually become England," Max explained. "It's not an island yet; it's physically connected to what will one day become Europe. The climate is much warmer in this time."

"Wow," was all Joe could say.

Max shrank the Silver Sphere and put it back in his pocket. I'm afraid the trekker doesn't work this far in the past," he told Joe, "so we'll have to walk."

"Where are we going?" Joe asked.

Max pointed at the horizon. "Inside that volcano."

Joe couldn't help but gulp. "Oh."

They'd been walking for about ten minutes when they heard a noise behind them. Grabbing Joe's arm, Max pulled him off the path to hide behind a tree. When Joe looked back at where they'd been walking, he saw the most amazing scene.

There was a small herd of enormous dinosaurs walking towards a large lake (much bigger than the one they'd seen when they'd first arrived).

Max explained that it was a Titanosaurus herd. "They are harmless," he told Joe. "They're herbivores, which means they only eat leaves."

Despite this, however, they kept their distance to avoid being trampled and squashed by the herd.

An hour later, the friends were still walking and it was starting to get dark. "We should stop for the night," suggested Max, "as it will be too dangerous to travel in the dark." He explained that, even though they hadn't seen any other dinosaurs on their journey, that didn't mean they weren't around.

Joe agreed. He knew they had to be careful in this time.

Max took something out of his pocket and threw it against the ground. There was a loud bang and, once again, the large Silver Sphere appeared. "It will be better if you sleep in the Silver Sphere," Max told Joe as he set up a hammock inside the small transport device. "I'll keep watch outside – just to be on the safe side."

Joe nodded, taking one last glance around him before making his way inside the Silver Sphere.

***

Joe had been sleeping soundly all night when, suddenly, he heard a loud roar. He bolted upright as the doors to the time machine slid open and Max ran inside.

"I think we have a problem!" he shouted.

A video monitor rose from the floor and, peering at it, Joe could see what the problem was. There was a giant dinosaur right outside the Silver Sphere. "What is it?" he screamed.

"It's a Tyrannosaurus rex," Max replied.

The T-Rex started sniffing at the Silver Sphere. It then started nudging it with its head. Each time the T-Rex nudged the Silver Sphere, it moved forward a little, and Joe could see from the monitor that each nudge was pushing the Sphere closer and closer to the edge of a small cliff.

"Strap in!" screamed Max.

As fast as they could, they sat in the chairs and put their seatbelts on, just in time to see the edge of the cliff approaching.

The T-Rex nudged the Sphere once more and, with that, it fell over the edge.

***

The Silver Sphere had landed in a fast-flowing river and was now being carried downstream at speed. Joe and Max were being spun around as if they were inside a large washing machine.

"How do we stop?!" screamed Joe.

"We need to wait until the flow of the river slows down," Max told him.

Joe gritted his teeth as he held onto his chair, hoping they'd be stopping soon – he was beginning to feel a little sick.

After what seemed like an eternity, the Sphere did in fact start to slow down and, eventually, it stabilised.

"What happened?" asked Joe.

"The river's getting calmer," Max explained.

The Silver Sphere was now floating gently down the river and, before long, Max had managed to regain full control and was able to steer them towards the shore.

Joe and Max disembarked from the sphere, relieved that they'd got back to land.

Max shrunk the sphere and put it back in his pocket. "Are you okay?"

Joe didn't respond. He was too busy thinking about how unbelievable this day had been. If he hadn't seen, heard, felt, and smelt the landscape around him, he would have definitely thought he was dreaming.

There was one good thing about their unplanned river cruise: it had taken them closer to the volcano.

"How do you know that the pyramids are in the volcano?" asked Joe, looking up at the huge mountain.

Max turned to face Joe. "I don't know for sure, but the sensor in the Silver Sphere shows that Dardan is in this time, and the volcano looks exactly like the place on my planet where he comes from. It's undeniably the type of place he'd hide the pyramids."

They continued walking for most of the day before they were forced to stop. The undergrowth in the jungle was getting thicker and thicker and, as such, the journey was getting more and more difficult.

"I'll climb to the top of that tree," said Max, pointing at an enormous oak tree right in front of them.

As Max climbed, Joe waited patiently but nervously on the ground. Every sound he heard coming from the jungle seemed like it was being made by something that wanted to eat him (and there were certainly lots of hungry creatures in this jungle).

Suddenly, there was a loud roaring sound that made the hairs on Joe's arms stand on end. Turning towards the direction of the roar, he started to panic. It sounded far away, but as far as Joe was concerned, it wasn't far enough.

Joe looked up at the oak tree to see Max climbing down. "Hurry up!" he hissed.

"Come with me," instructed Max – as calm as ever – as he started walking further into the jungle.

Joe followed. He was relieved that Max was back and that they were getting further away from the roaring sound.

A few moments later, Max said excitedly, "You're not going to believe what I've just seen!"

As they passed through a heavy section of jungle and into a clearing, Joe realised what Max was so excited about: in the trees at the other side of the clearing was an enormous treehouse.

***

Patrick and Lily had lived in a treehouse in this jungle for almost a whole year now. Along with their parents, they had built a safe spot to live in the middle of this dangerous place.

They had arrived here accidently, following one of their dad's experiments with a type of transporter he'd invented.

Professor Robinson had thought he'd invented a machine that could transport someone anywhere in the world instantaneously. He was so confident in the safety and effectiveness of the machine that he'd decided his family (him, Mrs Robinson, and the twins, Patrick and Lily) should go somewhere exotic.

At first, he thought that the transporter had worked – they had definitely arrived somewhere exotic! It was only after they saw their first dinosaur that Professor Robinson realised he'd made a terrible mistake. And, to make matters worse, the transporter was now broken – with no way to repair it. They were stuck. It was only thanks to Mrs Robinson, an architect, that they had the skills to build their treehouse.

The first few weeks had been scary. This part of the jungle didn't get that many dinosaurs, but occasionally one or two would pass through. The family had slept in the transporter for those first few weeks, but the professor soon realised it was too dangerous to spend too long on the ground. If a Tyrannosaurus had passed by, they would have been eaten. So, they got building and moved into the treehouse just six weeks after arriving.

Patrick was the older of the two twins (but only by 25 minutes). At 5'4, he was tall for his age, with longish blond hair. He desperately wanted a haircut but there was a distinct lack of hairdressers in the Cretaceous period. He wore a battered pair of blue jeans and a white t-shirt.

At 5'1, Lily was much shorter. She also had long blonde hair, which she constantly tied back into a ponytail, and she wore a pair of tracksuit bottoms and a blue t-shirt.

When they'd left their home the family hadn't packed any clothes, as the trip was only supposed to be for a day. The lack of clothes was a constant source of frustration for the twins.

"What are you up to?" Lily snapped at Patrick.

"None of your business!" Patrick hissed.

Patrick and Lily loved being brother and sister but, like many siblings, they did bicker a lot. After all, there really wasn't much to do in this treehouse, and it wasn't safe to travel too far into the jungle.

Patrick started running in and out of Lily's bedroom, making growling and roaring noises.

"Stop that!" Lily demanded. "You're scaring me."

"Don't be silly," said Patrick, "I'm just messing around."

Lily glanced at him with a look of anger and disappointment and, as usual, Patrick started to feel guilty. He immediately apologised and sat down next to his sister.

The two siblings had just turned 13 and had celebrated this milestone birthday at the top of a tree in a dinosaur-infested jungle. It wasn't exactly where they'd expected to become teenagers.

Suddenly, they heard a loud roar.

Patrick quickly stood up and pulled a cord that was hanging from the ceiling, causing the ringing of a bell to echo throughout the treehouse. A second later, the professor and Mrs Robinson ran into Lily's bedroom.

"What is it?" shrieked Mrs Robinson.

The twins both replied in unison, "Dinosaur!"

Professor Robinson pulled out a pair of binoculars and scanned the clearing. After a second or two, he turned back to his family with a look of shock. He then handed the binoculars to Patrick, who also looked out at the clearing.

Patrick couldn't believe what he was seeing. He turned away

and rubbed his eyes. Then he turned back and looked again.

"What is it?" asked Lily.

"It… it looks like two boys!"

***

Joe and Max cautiously approached the treehouse. It was just so completely unexpected, what with it being in the middle of a jungle in the time of the dinosaurs. It simply shouldn't have been here.

"Is there anybody there?" shouted Max.

There was no response.

They reached the bottom of the tree and glanced around. It didn't look like there was any way of getting up to the treehouse.

Suddenly, another loud roar came bellowing out of the jungle. Whatever it was, it was getting closer.

They both turned towards the direction of the roar just in time to see an enormous Tyrannosaurus walk out from the jungle and into the clearing.

The gigantic dinosaur surveyed the clearing, soon noticing an extremely vulnerable Joe and Max standing by the tree. Without hesitating it lurched towards the tree, gaining speed and momentum with every step.

Joe suggested that they try to climb the tree, but before Max could respond a rope ladder dropped down from above.

They hesitated for a few moments.

"We have no idea who's up there," cautioned Max.

In return, Joe squealed, "Yes, but we know what's down here!"

By now the T-Rex was getting extremely close. They simply had no other choice.

So, Joe and Max climbed up the rope ladder as quickly as they could. When they reached the top of the ladder, they climbed into the treehouse just as the tree started trembling and rocking. The T-Rex had rammed into the tree headfirst and was now lying unconscious on the ground below.

"Are you okay?" asked Lily.

"Yes thanks," replied Max.

The Robinson family just stood there, staring at Joe and Max in shock.

"What are you doing here?" asked Professor Robinson.

"Really!" said Mrs Robinson, shaking her head. "Have we forgotten our manners? Boys, please, take a seat and get your breath back. Then you can tell us – whenever you're ready."

Joe and Max gratefully sat down and explained the whole story to the Robinsons. The professor then told Joe and Max how his family had arrived in this place.

"Can you take us back to 2021?" asked Mrs Robinson.

Max looked at her and replied, "Of course we can."

The Robinson family cheered in unison, unable to believe their luck.

"Thank you so much!" gushed Patrick, who was practically jumping up and down in his excitement.

Max turned to look at the volcano in the distance as he explained that they couldn't, however, go back to 2021 just yet. "Joe and I need to complete our mission first. We need to find Dardan and the stolen pyramids."

"We'll help you," said the professor, "but it will be dark soon and we also need to wait for that dinosaur to leave. You can both stay here tonight."

"Thank you," said Joe. He didn't fancy sleeping on the ground with the T-Rex around.

The professor reminded Joe of the teachers at his school; he looked a bit nerdy with his suit and thick glasses. He had a bushy beard and shoulder length hair. Mrs Robinson had long blonde hair and was wearing shorts and a jacket. Even though they had been trapped in a jungle, they both looked very smart. Joe thought they must be in their early forties. He instinctively knew that he could trust them.

As night fell over the jungle, the six visitors of this strange land sat down for dinner together. Over the past year the Robinson family had learnt exactly what was safe to eat, and so the group were able to enjoy a tasty vegetarian meal.

After dinner, when everybody else was sleeping, Joe stood on the balcony at the highest point of the treehouse and looked out over the jungle. He couldn't believe where he was. It seemed so peaceful now. He couldn't tell if the T-Rex was still on the ground below, but at least there were no more scary noises.

For just a moment it felt like paradise, but then a disturbing thought crossed his mind.

He started to think about how worried his mum and dad would be, even though Max had reassured him they'd return at the exact same time that they'd left. No one would even know they'd been gone.

After taking one last look across the beautiful jungle landscape, Joe lay down, closed his eyes, and drifted off to sleep.

Chapter 4

By the time morning broke, the T-Rex had gone.

After a quick breakfast, Joe, Max, and the Robinson family packed up all their essential belongings, left the treehouse, and started the walk to the volcano.

As they went, Joe looked up and noticed something in the sky. "What's that?" he asked.

Max glanced up at the seemingly stationary streak of light in the sky.

"That is the Chicxulub impactor[2]" said Max. "It's the meteor that caused the extinction of the dinosaurs. That must be how Dardan was able to store up enough energy to steal the pyramids."

Lily stopped in her tracks. "What?! How long until it hits?"

"Don't worry," replied Max. "It looks like it won't be for another couple of days. We have plenty of time."

Lily nodded, trying to calm down, but she couldn't help but look up again at the ominous streak of light.

The path was long and exhausting, but the closer they got to the volcano the less dense the jungle became. They continued making good progress and, soon enough, they arrived at the base of the volcano.

"Now we need to find an entrance. There should be a cave somewhere," Max told the group.

The group spread out, looking for a way to access the inside of the volcano, and it wasn't long before they found the entrance to a cave.

"I think it would be safer if you all waited here," said Max. "I'll go in alone and meet you back here shortly."

"Absolutely not!" replied the professor. "We need to stick together. If anything happens to you, we'll all be stuck here," he added.

"And there are only a couple of days until the meteor crashes and causes the extinction of the dinosaurs," Lily reminded him.

Max looked at the group. "Okay, we stick together – but if it gets too dangerous then you'll have to find somewhere safe to hide." He took the Silver Sphere out of his pocket and gave it to the professor. "You should look after this. If anything happens to me, you just need to throw it and it will activate. The controls are self-explanatory. And please make sure Joe gets home as well."

"Thank you," replied the professor, "but I won't need to use it – we're all going to leave together."

Now that they were all in agreement, they headed into the cave. The temperature was very high inside, and the walk was uncomfortable and sticky. They carried on walking for ten minutes or so before they reached an opening. Then, cautiously, they all

2. Named after the place in Mexico where the crater from the meteor impact is located.

entered to find themselves in what appeared to be a desert.

"What? Where are we?" asked Joe. "Did we make a wrong turn somewhere?"

"No," replied Max. "We are in the right place. We've walked right through the volcano."

Joe, who was feeling both brave and curious, decided to walk into the desert. As he did so, he turned to his right and almost fell to the floor in shock.

When the others followed, they realised that Max's hunch had been correct: directly in front of them – in the most unlikely time and place – were the Giza Pyramids.

"What do we need to do?" Joe asked Max.

Max explained to the group that he needed to find the machine Dardan had used to transport the landmarks.

Before he could say anything else, however, a loud squawking sound came at them from above. They all looked up to see a flock of flying dinosaurs.

The professor knew exactly what they were. "They look like pterodactyls. Run!

The pterodactyls swooped down and picked up Joe, Max, and the Robinsons before the group even knew what was happening. The flock then flew up into the air before swooping back down into the volcano caves. The flying dinosaurs rushed through passages and passages of the cave system before swooping down again and gently dropping their passengers into a deep cavern.

Once the pterodactyls had flown off, the group all stood up and looked around. The cavern was well lit and included a strange computer. It was eerily silent.

Joe realised that it looked just like the cave in which he had first met Max.

The silence was broken by a howling sound, which made Joe

and the Robinsons jump. This didn't, however, startle Max. He knew exactly who it was.

"It's Dardan," he warned.

*****

The reality of this moment was far scarier than Joe had imagined. As a two-legged, man-sized wolf creature walked towards the terrified group, he realised that nothing could have prepared him for this.

"Good to see you again, Maxelon," said Dardan. "Who are your friends?"

Max approached Dardan. "They are not a threat to you," he said calmly, "just let them go."

Dardan surveyed the group that were huddled together in front of him. "I haven't decided what I'm going to do yet," he announced. "For now, they will be my guests."

Just then, a noise started emanating from one of the passages – a marching kind of sound.

As it got louder, the professor pulled out the Silver Sphere and threw it on the ground. "Let's go!"

Just then, a green beam appeared from the central console and, before the Silver Sphere could expand, it was destroyed.

"No!" screamed Lily, while the others merely stared and gasped.

The sound of the marching grew louder, and – from out of the darkness – emerged something even scarier than Dardan: a whole group of bird-like blue and green dinosaurs with long necks and feathered arms, walking in unison on their two hind legs.

"Meet my army of Troodon[3] soldiers!" bragged Dardan.

3 a type of dinosaur

The dinosaurs rushed over and carried away the Robinson family before anyone could even try to move.

As they disappeared into the darkness, Joe shouted after them, "We'll save you!"

Dardan shook his head, laughing.

Now there was only Joe, Max, and Dardan left in the main cavern.

Max looked directly at Dardan. "What are you planning to do now?"

"As soon as I've harvested enough of the mystical power of the pyramids, I'm going to open a time portal and transport my army to the 21st century," Dardan explained, grinning. "My Wolfian friends will be joining me to take over this primitive planet. I must thank you, Maxelon, for the use of this Tamiran technology. The *Organatech* seeds have allowed me to build this wonderful console."

"We won't let that happen!" Max responded angrily.

Max grabbed Joe's hand and pulled him along, the two of them running down the passage that the Troodon army had used to take away the Robinsons.

"We need to use Dardan's time portal," Max panted as they ran. "We only have two days before the meteor crashes. I'll send you and the Robinsons home and then I'll deal with Dardan myself."

"That's not going to happen," replied Joe. "We're a team; you can't defeat Dardan on your own. Let's find somewhere to hide so we can come up with a plan."

***

Back in the main cavern, Dardan was standing at his control deck. He wasn't at all worried about Max and Joe. He knew his Troodon army would find them eventually.

What he needed now was patience. He didn't have enough power to open a portal to the future yet; the only thing with that much power would be the Chicxulub impactor combined with the power of the pyramids. So, now he had to wait for the meteor to enter the Earth's atmosphere. The energy released from it would give him enough power to transport his Troodon army into the future. He knew it wouldn't be long before he became the ruler of Earth.

Dardan looked at the monitor in front of him – it showed him exactly where his Troodon soldiers were. Leaning forward, he pushed a button on the console. This was the mind control button. It was this Wolfian technology that allowed him to control the Troodons.

Once again, the sound of marching could be heard coming down the passage, and – as the Troodon army emerged into the cavern – Dardan looked up, howled, and gave his most important order so far.

"Find Maxelon – and his friend."

Chapter 5

The sound of the marching Troodon army could be heard echoing throughout the volcano's network of passages and caves. It was an ominous sound, but it was helping Max and Joe to stay hidden. It wasn't, however, allowing them to find the Robinson family.

They had been hiding for several hours, and time was running out.

"We need to find them," said Max. "We need to move."

"What about Dardan and his army?" asked Joe.

Max looked towards the end of the passage they were in. "We need to stop him before we leave, but we need to rescue the Robinsons first."

Joe nodded.

Cautiously, the two unlikely friends walked towards the end of the passage and listened intently; it sounded like the Troodon soldiers were far away.

This was their chance. They needed to find the Robinsons, stop Dardan's evil scheme, and get back to the 21st century... all before the Chicxulub impactor hit.

"I think I can hear someone," whispered Joe.

Max nodded. The sound of talking could be heard ahead. "It's the Robinsons."

After walking for a few more minutes, they reached a small cave that was separated from the passage with bars over the entrance. It looked just like a dungeon. On the other side of the bars, they could see the Robinsons.

At the sight of Max and Joe, the Robinsons sighed in relief.

"It doesn't look like anybody's guarding this dungeon," said a confused Joe, glancing up and down the passageway.

The professor lowered his voice before replying, "There was a Troodon guard, but he left a couple of hours ago. I think the whole army is out there looking for you."

Max looked around for anything they could use to help the Robinsons escape. Finally, he noticed a pile of volcanic dust on the ground. *This looks interesting,* he thought. He blew onto the dust pile, revealing a button underneath, and when he pressed it the bars to the dungeon immediately sank into the ground.

"You did it!" said Lily excitably.

Suddenly, they realised they could hear the unmistakable marching sound of the approaching Troodon army. Not knowing what else to do, Max and Joe joined the Robinsons in the dungeon. As soon as they did, the bars rose again from the ground.

"Did you think it would be that easy?" boomed Dardan over a loudspeaker.

The prisoners looked at each other in horror as they realised what was happening.

The walls to the dungeon were closing in around them.

***

"Look around!" ordered Max. "Find a button or lever. There must be a way to stop the mechanism."

They all started looking around, trying not to panic – though that was easier said than done. The walls were moving quite slowly, but they all knew it wouldn't be long until they were completely crushed.

It was a terrifying thought.

After a few moments, Patrick noticed a hole in one of the walls outside the dungeon. "I've found a lever!" he screamed. He attempted to reach it, but it was too far away. "I can't get to it!"

The walls were getting much closer now, and the professor held out both his arms in an attempt to slow them down.

"Mum!" shouted Patrick. "Can you use your scarf to reach the lever?"

Mrs Robinson ran to the hole and, even though her hands were shaking, she managed to loop the scarf that had been in her jacket pocket over the lever. "It won't move!" she screamed, continuing to pull on the lever. It just wouldn't budge.

"Hold onto Mrs Robinson," said Max. "When she holds onto the lever, we'll pull her. Between us, we should have enough strength to move it."

So, Mrs Robinson pulled on the lever while the rest of the group (except for the professor, who was still trying to keep the walls from getting any closer) pulled her back. After a few seconds of suspense, the lever finally moved – and the walls stopped moving too.

"Ten more seconds and we'd have been squished!" gulped Lily.

There was no time to celebrate, though, as suddenly they felt a tremor beneath them. The floor was shaking; it seemed like the volcano was going to erupt.

"What's happening?" asked Joe.

"It's the meteor," said Max. "It's just crashed in Mexico. I must have misjudged the time of the collision."

"What?" asked Joe. "What does that mean?"

"It means we've only got an hour to get out."

"But how?" questioned the professor, still reeling from this news. "The Silver Sphere was crushed."

"We need to get to Dardan's main console. It can open a time portal," Max explained. "That's why he stole the pyramids. It will power up his console and allow him to travel through time."

Fortunately, the tremor had caused the bars to sink back into the ground, allowing them to run out of the dungeon.

"Follow me!" shouted Max. "I know where to go!"

***

By the time they reached the central cavern, Max estimated that they only had 15 minutes left until the devastation from the meteor would reach the volcano.

Unfortunately, Dardan and his army were already there.

"You're too late!" he cackled as they arrived in the cavern. "My army and I are now ready to take over the world, and there's nothing you can do about it!"

A second later, there was a bright flash of light and a portal opened. Dardan howled before following his army through.

As the portal closed, Max ran towards the control deck and pressed a collection of buttons. "I've returned the pyramids to their rightful place and time," he told the group. "It will be as if they never left. Now, we need to go."

As the volcano trembled and shook even more, rocks started falling all around the cavern.

Max pressed a few more buttons and then there was another bright flash. Another portal had opened. "Let's go!" he shouted.

They all rushed over to the portal and ran through.

Max was the last to enter, and as the portal closed the volcano exploded, showering the landscape with molten rock and lava.

***

Joe squinted as he emerged into the light. The Robinsons were next, and they were followed by Max. They all looked around, taking in their surroundings and blinking in the sudden daylight.

"We're in a field," said Lily. "Are we back home?"

"Not quite," said Max. "I didn't have time to set the exact coordinates. I had to stop Dardan getting to the 21st century so I changed his destination. I could only open our portal to the same time."

"So, when are we?" asked the professor noticing a camp in the distance.

Before Max could answer, they noticed a group of people approaching on horseback.

As the group got closer, Joe realised when they were. "Are they Roman legionaries?" he asked.

"Yes," replied Max.

"What's the year?" growled the professor.

Max looked at his friends and sighed. "It's the year AD 143."

Part 3: The Romans

Chapter 6

"*Quid agitis?*" said the leader of the Roman battalion as they reached the group.

The friends all looked at each other in confusion.

"Pardon?" replied the professor.

The leader of the battalion looked directly at him. "*Secus non tutum. Monstra hic sunt. Suntne liberi tui?*"

Joe realised what was going on. "They're speaking Latin," he told the others. "That's the language the ancient Romans spoke. We learnt about it in school."

Max started rummaging in his pocket, eventually pulling out a handful of small seeds. "These are called Lingua worm eggs," he explained to the group. "They live on my planet. Put them in your ears. They will translate any known language. The Romans will be able to understand us as well."

"In our ears?" asked a concerned Lily.

"Yes," replied Max. "Don't worry – it's very safe. They will hatch after about three weeks and then the worm will crawl out. Until then, you will be able to understand any language."

Joe thought this sounded like a disgusting thing to be voluntarily putting in their ears, but they didn't really have a choice.

"What are you doing?" repeated the leader of the Roman battalion.

"That's better. We can understand you now," said the professor. "Could you repeat everything you just said to us?"

"It's not safe. There are monsters here."

The professor looked at Max. "He must be talking about the Troodons. We're in the right place."

"Are they your children?" asked the Roman, gesturing at the twins.

"Yes," the professor replied quickly. "They are with us."

Without saying another word, the Roman legionary returned to his horse and led his group away, leaving Max, Joe, and the Robinsons alone in the middle of the field.

"We are in roughly same place that we were in the Cretaceous period," Max informed them. "That means that Dardan's cave will be around here somewhere. It will be buried, but it'll be here somewhere. We just need to find it before Dardan does."

The professor looked across the field at a nearby forest. "We need to find somewhere less public until we can figure out what to do. Let's head into that forest."

With everyone in agreement, they all headed into the woods, making their way deep into the thick undergrowth.

After a while, Joe heard a sound. "Listen!" he whispered.

They all stopped in their tracks and, suddenly, the ground beneath them gave way.

A couple of seconds later, Joe stood up and looked around. The fall had winded him, but he was otherwise uninjured. He turned to check on the others and, once again, he found that he couldn't believe what he was seeing.

He was standing directly in front of Stonehenge.

***

Slowly, the others – who had just about recovered from the fall – all stood up.

"What's it doing here?" asked a bewildered Joe.

They had found themselves in a huge cavern – not Stonehenge's usual home.

Max approached the enormous monument, studying it carefully as he walked around every stone. "This has not been transported through time, but it has been moved from its original site in Salisbury," he told them. "Dardan must have already found the cave and transported Stonehenge here. Its mystical power – combined with the residual power of the Chicxulub impactor – might be enough to open another portal."

Lily looked excitably at Max. "So, we can get home?"

"I think so," replied Max. "As long as we find the cave."

The relieved group started studying their surroundings more closely.

"There's an entrance!" exclaimed Patrick, a few seconds later.

There was indeed a large opening in front of them. It looked like it led into a cave system.

"This must be Dardan's cave," said Max. "Come on – let's have a look."

Together, they headed into the cave and walked towards the end of a long passage. As they reached the end of the passage, they once again found themselves in Dardan's cave.

"It looks terrible," said Joe, glancing around at the crumbling rocks and piles of debris.

"Remember," Max told him, "that even though it feels like only an hour or so for us, this place has actually been buried for millions of years." He approached the central console. Like the cave, it had also seen better days, but some of the lights were still blinking.

"There was enough residual power left to transport Stonehenge here," Max told the group, "and I think we'll all be able to get home, but it needs repairing first."

The professor looked at Max. "Is it easy to figure out?" He studied the console. "I think I could fix this. I am an inventor, after all."

"Great idea," replied Max. "We also need to find Dardan and the Troodon army. We can't leave them in Roman Britain."

Joe looked at Max, frowning. "Why don't we just wait here?

They'll come back eventually."

The professor had immediately realised why this wasn't a good idea. "We can't let a dinosaur army go rampaging around the place; it's too dangerous. We need to find them as soon as possible."

Max agreed. "Why don't you and your family stay here and try to fix the console? Joe and I will look for Dardan."

"But what will we do if we find them?" asked an understandably scared Joe.

"Honestly, I'm not sure yet," replied Max, shrugging. "I'm figuring this out as we go. Don't worry, though – I won't let you come to any harm."

Max turned to the professor. "You'll need to hide if Dardan returns."

So, while the Robinson family stayed in the cave to repair the console, Max and Joe headed back out into the cavern.

"There must be a way up. How did Dardan and the Troodons do it?" Joe pondered out loud.

Max turned to look at Stonehenge again, noticing a steep uphill path just behind it. "I think I've found a way up."

They started the steep walk up and, before too long, found themselves back in the forest.

"Let's head into the town," said Max.

Joe nodded, trying to ignore the butterflies swarming around his stomach.

72

Chapter 7

The screams could be heard for miles around.

"Run!"

"What are they?"

"They're monsters!"

The Troodon army had just arrived in the small town of Venonis and the population were understandably terrified. The people who lived in Roman times had never seen or even heard of such a thing as a dinosaur.

The Troodons, however, weren't hurting anyone; they were just herding the townspeople into the centre of a park.

As the park became more and more crowded, a battalion of Roman legionaries arrived, firing furiously at the Troodon army with their bows and arrows.

"Charge!" shouted the centurion[4] of the battalion.

In unison, the legionaries ran towards the Troodon army with their swords out, ready to attack. The Troodon army immediately turned away from the townspeople and towards the approaching legionaries.

"Stop!" said a voice from above.

The townspeople and legionaries looked up to see a wolf-like creature floating on a hovering board.

"My name is Dardan," he told his captive audience, "and these are my friends. We are not here to harm you. We just want to help you."

"How can you help us?" asked the centurion in his loud, booming voice.

Dardan hovered gently down to the ground and landed directly in front of the centurion. "We have travelled through space and time," he explained. "We are trying to capture a group of dangerous prisoners."

"Why should we trust you?" shouted one of the townspeople. "You look like a monster!"

Dardan stared directly at the crowd. "Yes, I'm sure we must look very unusual to you, but remember – you also look strange to us. To show you that we can be trusted, I will give you the gift of flight."

Suddenly, a small portal opened in the sky, out of which fell hundreds of hovering boards just like the one Dardan was using. He had used the remainder of his *Organa-tech* seeds to create these flying machines.

"This is my gift to you," he announced. "Just imagine how much more powerful the Roman Empire will be with the power of flight. Your armies will be unbeatable, and the Empire will last for eternity."

The centurion looked down at the pile of hovering boards on the ground.

4. Commander

"Stand on one," said Dardan.

Cautiously, the centurion stood on one of the boards and immediately started to hover in the air.

"Lean forward to move. You won't fall off," instructed Dardan.

The centurion nervously leant forward and started moving through the air, laughing in delight. The board was easy to use and, before long, he was travelling around the centre of town at high speed.

"How do I go higher?" he asked.

"Stand on the button to your left," replied Dardan.

The board started to gain height and, in a matter of seconds, the centurion was soaring high above the people and dinosaurs.

"What do you want from us?" shouted the centurion as he hovered over to Dardan.

Dardan looked at the townspeople. "I want to be your leader."

***

"Not too far now," said Max, pointing at a sign stating that Venonis was three miles away.

Picking up their pace a little, Max and Joe continued walking in the direction of the town.

"We must hope that we've beaten Dardan and his army there. We need to warn them about him," said Max.

Joe nodded in response. The closer they got to Venonis, the more nervous he was becoming.

The road into town was deserted; they hadn't come across anyone during their journey so far, and Max was starting to worry. "This is unusual. Let's stop and wait for a few minutes."

Joe's nerves were most definitely growing. He'd seen so much over the last few days, and while it had all been amazing, it had also been pretty frightening. He was starting to wish he'd never explored that unexploded bomb site.

The path into town had been built right through the middle of the forest, and Max and Joe decided it would be safer to wait in the forest for a while, where they could hide behind trees and rocks if they needed to.

Suddenly, they heard a loud whooshing sound from above, and they both looked up to see a Roman legionary hovering in the sky. He held something up to his mouth, and the distinctive sound of a military trumpet blasted out into the air.

"They're here!" shouted the legionary.

Before Max and Joe could get away, they found themselves surrounded by Roman legionaries.

"Stay calm," Max whispered to Joe as the soldiers walked up to them with ancient-looking handcuffs.

Just moments later, the legionaries were marching into town with Max and Joe chained up as their prisoners. As they arrived in town, they noticed that the streets here were deserted too. They continued until they reached the park.

The park was also eerily silent. Here, Max and Joe were unchained, placed in the centre of the park, and once again surrounded by legionaries. There was no chance of escape.

"Where is everyone?" a scared Joe whispered to Max.

The trumpet was heard once again, and all the Romans knelt down on the ground as the unmistakable whooshing sound of a hovering board sounded from above. Max, Joe, and all the kneeling legionaries looked up.

"Good to see you again, Maxelon." Dardan hovered down to the ground, landing right in front of Max and Joe. "I see you've met my army."

"Your army?" asked Max.

"Yes," replied Dardan. "I've already explained to them that you are a dangerous escaped prisoner. They have agreed that, in return for your capture, I will provide technology that will ensure the Roman Empire lasts forever. They've also agreed to make me the leader of this town."

Max looked over at all the kneeling legionaries. "Let me speak to your leader. You've been lied to. Dardan is the criminal; he followed me here from my planet."

The legionaries did not respond. Instead, they just looked at Dardan.

"Your lies will not work here," said Dardan. "Where are your other friends?"

Max quickly responded, "They're not here. We left them in the Cretaceous period."

"He's lying!" shouted one of the legionaries. "We saw him with his friends earlier today."

Dardan looked at the legionary. "Thank you. What is your name?"

The excited legionary quickly replied, "Verissimus."

"Well, Verissimus, you will be rewarded," Dardan informed him. "Please, all stand."

The kneeling legionaries all stood up as the unforgettable sound of the marching Troodon army could be heard approaching in the distance.

Dardan stared at the legionaries standing in front of him, before focusing on the one who had spoken. "Verissimus, you will lead my Troodon army."

In response, Verissimus bowed.

As the marching sound grew louder, Max and Joe looked at each other. This hadn't exactly worked out as planned.

The Troodon army marched into the park. Max noticed that the dinosaurs were all wearing saddles.

"Verissimus, take your pick," said Dardan.

Verissimus looked at each of the Troodons in front of him and made his choice. Climbing onto the green dinosaur, he sat in the saddle and looked around. At Dardan's command, the other legionaries chose a Troodon each and saddled up.

"I need you to transport these prisoners to Londinium!" ordered Dardan.

"Yes sir!" replied Verissimus.

Joe's stomach dropped.

***

"How's it going?" asked Lily.

The professor looked at the alien technology laid out in front of him. "Not too bad," he replied.

He was actually doing a very good job of making sense of the strange technology. He had already managed to reboot the main console, and it was showing him exactly where the Troodon army was. Now, he was trying to figure out how to switch off the mind control software Dardan was using to control the Troodons.

"We need to figure out how to send the Troodons back into the past before we switch off the mind control," he told the rest of his family. "It would be even worse to have wild, *uncontrolled* dinosaurs rampaging around Roman Britain."

Mrs Robinson looked at her husband, her eyebrows raised. "Well, why can't we control them? That way, we can make sure they don't hurt anybody before we're able to send them back home."

The professor smiled at his wife. "What a great idea! Where's Patrick?"

A moment later, Patrick appeared from one of the passages. "I'm here!"

The professor explained what they were planning to do and asked Patrick to help him. "We need to find the wireless mechanism for the mind control software so that Dardan no longer has control. *We* should then be able to control the Troodons from here at the console. What do you think?"

Patrick grinned. He loved working on inventions with his dad, and this was the most important project they'd ever been involved in.

Meanwhile, Lily and Mrs Robinson were watching the console monitor. The Troodons were still nowhere near the cave.

For the first time since being trapped in the Cretaceous period, the whole family was feeling a collective sense of hope.

"I think this is going to work!" exclaimed Lily. "We'll finally be able to go home!"

The professor nodded in agreement as he connected two circuits together.

Outside the cave, Stonehenge started to shake. The mystical power of the monument was powering up the alien technology.

Then, the whole console started vibrating.

"What's happening?" asked Lily in alarm.

"I'm not sure," admitted the professor, frowning.

As the vibrations started to subside, the console lit up. All the buttons were illuminated in either red, green, or amber.

"It's working!" exclaimed an excited Patrick.

One of the buttons was blinking, alternating between amber and green. Patrick felt himself drawn towards this blinking button and, before anyone could stop him, he reached out and pushed it.

'No!" shouted Lily, Mrs Robinson, and the professor all at once.

Instantly, the cave began to tremble. This seemed like a very familiar feeling to the Robinson family and, before they could react, a portal opened directly in front of them.

They immediately heard a loud roar.

The portal had opened a pathway back to the Cretaceous period, and now a T-Rex was walking directly towards them.

"The console memory must have opened a portal back to the last time period it was activated in," suggested the professor, desperately trying to think.

As the T-Rex got closer, the professor pressed the same button Patrick had pushed just moments earlier. The portal closed just as the dinosaur started roaring again.

"We've done it!" said Patrick. "Max will be able to set the correct coordinates and we'll be able to get home!"

The professor, however, was not quite as excited. He'd just noticed some movement on the monitor.

The Troodons were heading back to the cave.

Chapter 8

"They've managed to get my console working!" shouted an angry Dardan, realising that Maxelon's friends were far more clever than he'd given them credit for. He ordered a battalion of Troodons and Romans to get back to the cave. "They cannot be allowed to stop me! I must become the ruler of the Earth!" He simply couldn't allow them to break his mind control of the Troodons.

A short distance away, Max and Joe had been caged up in a cart, and were now waiting for Verissimus to take them to Londinium. Though they hadn't heard what he'd said, they'd realised that something had upset Dardan and they suspected that the Robinsons had made progress in the cave.

"Legionaries, let's go!" ordered Verissimus.

A second later, the cart began to move. It was being pulled by two Troodons.

"We need to get out of this cage," whispered Max. "I've got an idea." He reached down to his belt and pulled out a small, round device.

"What's that?" asked Joe.

"Watch," replied Max. He pressed a button on the small device and, suddenly, the two Troodons who were pulling the cart stopped moving. "Hold on," Max whispered to Joe.

The two Troodons accelerated away from the rest of the soldiers, causing the cart to rock back and forth as their speed increased.

"What's happening?" asked Joe.

"I've broken the link between Dardan and these two dinosaurs," replied Max. "It won't last long, but hopefully it will be long enough."

As the speed increased, the cart began to break up; the wood was cracking and splitting and, soon enough, Max and Joe fell through the bottom. The back wheels just missed them as the cart continued on its high-speed journey.

They ran into the nearby woods just in time to see the two Troodons stop running and begin walking back to the other soldiers.

"Why didn't you do that before?" asked Joe.

"I couldn't," Max explained. "This device will only work once, and only on a couple of the dinosaurs." He threw the device onto the ground. "Now we need to get back to the cave."

***

"What are we going to do?" asked Mrs Robinson.

"I've got a plan," replied the professor. "I'm going to send the Troodons back to the past. I just need to figure out how to change the destination time. I don't want to send them to the end of the Cretaceous period. I'll send them back 100 years earlier."

"We also need to figure out how to break the mind control as well," Patrick reminded him.

Together, the professor and Patrick started frantically looking at the console for a way to change the date. The portal button was still blinking, ready for someone to press it. Instead, the professor pushed the button to the left of it.

Lily, who had been looking at the monitor, noticed an option menu appear. "Look at this!" she said to her family.

The monitor was now displaying a 'Choose Date' option.

"It's in English," said Mrs Robinson. "The worms in our ears must help us read languages as well as hear them."

By now the sound of marching could be clearly heard in the distance.

"They're coming!" shouted a terrified Lily.

The professor typed in a date during the Cretaceous period that was 100 years earlier than the time they'd been stuck there. "That's done," he told the others.

"So now we need to break the mind control," said Mrs Robinson.

The marching of the approaching army was getting louder and louder, and the professor was frantically looking for a way to stop the mind control of the Troodons when, suddenly, Max and Joe ran into the cave.

"Well done!" shouted Max as he approached the console. "We managed to get ahead of the army."

Reaching out, he pressed three buttons together at the exact same moment that the army marched into the cave.

The Troodons all threw the Romans off their backs and, as the Roman legionaries fell onto the ground, the dinosaurs turned towards them and started to growl.

"The mind control is broken!" shouted Max. "We need to get the Troodons into the portal and away from the Romans immediately – otherwise, they'll eat them!"

Max pushed another button before pressing the blinking portal button. "This portal is specifically programmed for the Troodons. It will automatically pull them towards it," he explained.

The cave began to shake, and the portal opened.

Within seconds, the Troodons had been pulled away from the terrified Roman legionaries and into the portal.

It wasn't over yet, though, as the rest of the Troodon army were pulled into the cave and through the portal from all around the local area. The Roman legionaries who had already been thrown from their saddles by the now free Troodons watched in amazement as the strange monsters were picked up by an invisible force before disappearing into the distance.

As the last Troodon vanished into the portal, Max pressed the blinking button again and the portal closed instantly.

"They've gone," said Max as the Roman legionaries ran out of the cave. "Now I need to get you all home."

Joe looked at Max. "What about Dardan?"

"I need to get him back to Proxima Centauri b. Now that the console is fully operational, I might be able to get us both back there." Max looked at the Robinson family. "Let's get you home first."

He typed 2nd February 2021 into the console, which then appeared on the monitor in front of them. He then, once again, pressed the blinking button. The cave began to shake, and another portal opened.

"This will get you back to the correct time, and we're only a few miles from where you first arrived in the past," explained Max.

The professor gathered his family together and smiled at Max and Joe. "Thank you for all your help. Please come visit us when you return to the future."

The rest of the family all said their goodbyes and then walked towards the portal, vanishing through it one by one.

As soon as they'd all passed through, Max closed the portal, typed 10th January 2022 into the console, and pressed the blinking button.

"It's time for you to go home too," he said to Joe.

Joe was reluctant to leave Max here on his own, but he was also desperate to get back home. Besides, he was confident that Max would be able to get back to his home now.

The portal opened, and Joe gave Max a hug. "Please keep in touch," he told him.

"Of course," replied Max.

Joe had just started walking towards the portal when, suddenly, it disappeared.

Max looked at the console in horror. The screen was blank.

Before Joe could ask what the problem was, they both heard a chilling – but all too familiar – howl.

***

Dardan glided into the central cavern on his hovering board, flanked by a large battalion of Roman legionaries. "I'm afraid I can't let you leave!" he bellowed.

Joe stood behind Max. "What are you going to do to us?" he asked.

Dardan looked directly at Joe and laughed. "You will stay here as my prisoners… forever."

Max stepped forward, staring angrily at Dardan as he shouted, "I won't let you keep Joe here! He needs to get home to his family! I'll stay."

Dardan stepped off his hovering board, walked past Max and Joe, and approached the console. He typed in a code and the blinking portal light went dark. "There will be no more time travelling today."

Max joined Dardan at the console. "What is your plan?" he

asked him. "You wanted to invade the future and rule the world."

Dardan sighed. "Yes, well… you ruined that plan. You returned the pyramids back to the future, so I no longer have the power to transport a whole army. Stonehenge has some power, but nowhere near enough for my original plan. The pyramids do exist in this time, but I've already exhausted their mystical power."

"So, what is your plan?" asked Max, genuinely curious.

"I am going to stay here for a few years," Dardan explained. "I can easily rule this primitive Earth. Then, once I have become a historical legend, I will travel back to the 21st century to be welcomed back as ruler of Earth."

Suddenly, the Roman legionaries started walking towards Joe.

"Meet my new army," said Dardan with a snarl.

Clearly, the legionaries were now under Dardan's control; when he pulled out a small remote control from his pocket and pressed a button, the legionaries pulled out their swords and pointed them at Joe and Max.

"Come with us," they all said in unison.

Joe was getting scared again. "They're like zombies," he whispered.

As the Romans continued marching towards Joe, the cave started to shake and vibrate again.

"What's going on?" shouted Dardan.

Before he could say anything else, a portal opened in the cave. This one, however, was nothing to do with Max or Dardan.

A familiar squawking sound could be heard coming from the world beyond the portal, and then – to the surprise of everyone in the cave – four pterodactyls came flying out. And they were not alone. They were being ridden by people.

A shout of "Geronimo!" could be heard just as one of the pterodactyls swooped down and grabbed Dardan's mind control remote, crushing it in its beak.

"No!" shouted Dardan.

The legionaries, who were now free of Dardan's mind control, immediately ran out of the cave.

The pterodactyls landed and their human passengers disembarked. Max, Joe, and Dardan could barely believe what they were seeing.

It was an older Lily, Patrick, and their parents.

***

This unexpected turn of events had distracted Dardan, which Max quickly took advantage of; with the help of the professor, he had soon restrained him. The pterodactyls stepped forwards then, carefully watching over Dardan – who had now found himself as Max's prisoner.

"What's going on?" asked Joe.

Lily and Patrick stepped forward. They were now 16 years old.

"It's been three years since we saw you," Lily explained, "though it must seem like just a few minutes to you."

Joe nodded, speechless.

The professor walked towards Joe. "When we arrived back in 2021, we realised immediately that there was something wrong," he explained. "Stonehenge was still in this location. And Dardan's supporters had been ruling the world since the Roman times."

Mrs Robinson spoke next. "The history books showed that assisted human flight had existed since AD 143."

"And at school, we learnt that the final dinosaur sighting was in Britain during the Roman times," added Lily.

"How did you manage to get back here?" asked Max. "To this time?"

The professor responded, "I used the knowledge I'd gained from accidentally building my own time machine and from repairing the technology in this cave to help me create a portable time machine. It took me three years to build it, but it lets me open a portal to any time I want."

"And the pterodactyls?" asked Max.

"In the future, all Dardan's followers have mind control devices," the professor explained. "I found the instructions on the internet and developed my own. Then we went back to the Cretaceous period, snuck into Dardan's cave, and freed all the pterodactyls he was controlling. We plan to send them back to a few years before the meteor crashes once we've rescued you both."

Dardan had listened carefully to this story, and he was pleased that his plan had worked. He still intended to make it happen and he still had one card up his sleeve.

"What's the plan then?" asked the professor.

"I'm going to take Dardan back to our planet where he will be returned to prison," Max told them. "I've been stuck on Earth for too long now; I want to go home. Can you take Joe back to his time?"

"Of course," said the professor.

"When you return home, everything will be back to normal," Max said with a smile.

The positivity in the cave was suddenly interrupted by a loud whooshing sound. Dardan looked up and grinned.

"I'm here, sir!" said a voice from above.

It was Verissimus.

And he was leading an army of flying Roman legionaries.

***

The legionaries quickly surrounded Max, Joe, and the Robinsons. However, Dardan was still being guarded by the four pterodactyls.

"How are you controlling these Romans?" asked Max. "Your mind controller has been destroyed!"

"These legionaries are my loyal soldiers. I don't need to use Wolfian technology to control them," replied Dardan as he stood up.

The four confused pterodactyls didn't know what to do; amidst all the confusion, they were regaining their free will. After a few moments they took off and flew down one of the passages. After eventually reaching the cave exit, they found themselves free to roam around Roman Britain.

Dardan was now free to get back to his control console. After running over, he flipped a switch on the main console and the portal light started blinking again.

"You still don't have enough power to transport a whole army," Max reminded him.

"I don't need to," Dardan responded. "I'm not sending my army through."

Max frowned, confused. "Then what are you doing?"

"I've given your request some thought. I'm sending your friends back home."

By now the Roman legionaries had completely filled the central cavern and there was no way to escape. Landing in front of the professor, Verissimus searched him and found the mind controller and portable time machine. He confiscated them both, then passed them over to Dardan, who destroyed them.

"You can return home," he said, "but without this technology. The future is yet to be written – it's very exciting. I hope you all enjoy it."

"What about Max?" asked Joe.

Dardan had his own plans for Max. "Maxelon will be staying here with me," he said as he pushed a button on the console. A bright strip of light appeared and shone directly onto Max. Then, to the complete horror of Joe and the Robinsons, Max immediately turned to stone.

"Just one of my new inventions. It's quite good, isn't it?" said Dardan, his face twisted into an ugly snarl.

Verissimus joined Dardan at the central console, and Dardan gave him the honour of pushing the blinking portal button. The familiar vibrations began and, once again, a portal opened.

"This will send you all back to your exact time zone. It will be as if you never left," Dardan told them. "I expect things might be a little different to how you remember, though."

The Robinson family were picked up and pulled through the portal, which then closed. There was a bright flash and a second portal opened.

Joe found himself being lifted off the ground before floating over to the portal, his eyes watering as he looked back at Max. As he entered the portal, he took one last look at his friend before a bright flash of light caused him to close his eyes.

Part 4: Home?

Chapter 9

Monday 10th January 2022

"Time to get up, Joseph!"

Joe opened his eyes to see his mum looking down at him.

"You don't want to be late for school," she said, before walking out of the bedroom.

Slowly, Joe got out of bed and looked around his room. Everything seemed normal. Had it all been a dream? He got dressed and went downstairs, where he was greeted enthusiastically by Milo.

"Milo, it seems like so long since I last saw you!" he exclaimed, picking up the cat and giving him a cuddle.

Joe was confused now. His adventure had felt so real... but maybe it had all just been one big strange dream?

The television was on in the kitchen, and the breakfast show was just as boring as it always had been. There was nothing on the news that seemed different or unusual. There wasn't even any mention of the disappearance of any monuments.

It must have been a dream, he thought as he packed up his bag and headed out for the day.

"Have a lovely day, Joseph," said Mrs Jackson as Joe walked out the door.

'Thanks, Mum," replied Joe.

"And watch out for birds!"

Joe thought this was a strange thing to say, but perhaps there had been some recent random bird attacks he wasn't aware of. He remembered seeing something on the television once, saying that some birds occasionally attack people who are carrying food.

The short walk to school was uneventful, with everything looking exactly the same as he remembered.

It was definitely a dream, he thought.

Joe perked up as he continued walking. Everything seemed normal, and he quite liked Mondays as he had double history. Even before his strange dream, it had always been his favourite subject.

"Alright Joe, how's things?"

At the sound of the voice, Joe turned around to see his best friend, Mohammed.

"How was your weekend?" asked Mohammed.

Joe wasn't sure how to answer. His dream had been so realistic that the weekend felt like a long time ago. "Hi Mo, oh… I didn't really do much. Bit boring. How about yours?"

Mo explained that his family had been to London. "It was good, but the birds were annoying – as usual."

"Really?" asked a confused Joe.

"Yes, but the police were able to disperse them by firing food into the air. That's all they want, isn't it?"

Joe nodded, though he had no idea what his friend was talking about.

A few minutes later Joe and Mo arrived at school and headed for their form group. The form tutor completed the register and then gave the group some messages. The messages were not very interesting and mainly about after-school clubs.

Just as Joe was getting ready to head to his first lesson of the day, a loud siren sounded. The tutor and the other students immediately stood up. Joe was the only person in the classroom still seated.

"What are you doing?" whispered Mo.

"What?" asked an even more confused Joe.

"Stand up!" bellowed Joe's form tutor.

Joe stood up and looked around. His classmates and tutor were now standing with their eyes closed. All of a sudden, a voice could be heard coming from a loudspeaker in the corner of the classroom.

"We are happy, we are happy, we are happy."

Joe was getting scared now. He was slowly becoming convinced that the last few days hadn't been a dream after all.

"We are grateful to our beloved leader for his kindness."

Everyone in the room was repeating this mantra, their eyes closed, their faces blank. It was like something out of a horror movie.

"We put our faith in the order of Verissimus."

Joe almost screamed when an image of Verissimus appeared on the ceiling. Everybody else had now opened their eyes and were cheering at the sight of the image. Joe looked outside the window and could see that everybody was doing the same thing. Cars had stopped and pedestrians were looking at the sky, at the image of Verissimus that had somehow been projected onto the clouds.

The siren sounded again, and Joe hurriedly sat down as the rest of his classmates took their seats in time for the lesson bell to ring.

"Have a great day, everyone!" said the tutor.

***

Joe needed to find Max. Would he still be in Dardan's cave? Would he be able to get to Max's cave? He decided that, after school, he would try to find the Robinsons; surely, they must be on social media.

He arrived at his history class and took his usual seat. The wall displays were showing pictures of Verissimus carrying out various heroic feats. There were also images of people who looked like Verissimus. Joe needed more information about the changes that had happened since he was last in this time.

"Can you tell us the story of our beloved leader please?" he asked his teacher.

"Of course," his teacher replied. "I'm very pleased you're showing so much interest."

The history teacher went on to explain that Verissimus had been a Roman hero. He had mastered the power of flight and had united the known world before discovering the new world of the Americas and Australia. The Order of Verissimus, he said, is passed down through a line of succession. Verissimus and his descendants, therefore, have been ruling the entire world since AD 143.

"The Order of Verissimus has kept us safe and happy for all these years," the teacher told the class. "It's hard to believe that, at one time, the people were not lucky enough to have our beloved leaders. We are so lucky to live on the United Planet of Verissium."

What? thought Joe. *The name of the planet has changed as well?!*

Joe was also wondering what had happened to Dardan, as there were no images of him anywhere, and his teacher had not mentioned him at all in the story of Verissimus.

A couple of hours later the lunchtime bell rang, and Joe and Mo

99

headed into the canteen.

"Why are you being so weird today?" asked Mo.

Joe wanted to tell his best friend what was going on, but he thought it would be better to keep the truth to himself – for now.

"I didn't sleep very well last night, that's all," said Joe, trying to sound casual as they trudged outside.

"Great. I'm glad you've not gone crazy," responded Mo.

Just as the two friends were sat having lunch in the schoolyard, an alarm sounded, echoing around the open space.

"Here we go again," sighed Mo, at the same time as Joe heard a loud squawking noise in the distance.

"We'd better take cover," said Mo. "We don't want to be the next John Hammond, do we?"

"Remind me what happened to John Hammond?" asked Joe.

Mo looked at Joe with bemusement. "You really are being weird today. He was taken by the birds and never seen again."

Joe was now beginning to realise what these 'birds' were. After all, he could still vividly remember the four pterodactyls who had escaped from Dardan's cave.

The squawking got louder and louder, and Joe looked up to see a large flock approaching.

"Run!" screamed one of the teachers.

The staff and students all ran into the canteen, and as they entered the large room Joe and Mo turned around and looked out of the window. The pterodactyls were circling the schoolyard. Occasionally, one of them would land and approach the canteen before realising they couldn't get in.

"Thank goodness we invested in bird-resistant glass," said one of the dinner ladies.

Joe noticed that several police vans were approaching the school. Each van had something that looked like a cannon placed on the roof.

It's David, thought Joe as he watched the police chief give the order to fire.

In unison, the cannons began firing all kinds of food into the air. The pterodactyls soon turned their attention to the food and, before long, they left the schoolyard. The alarm sounded again, and everybody headed outside.

Once school was over, Joe walked back down to the cave where he'd first met Max. He assumed that the unexploded bomb would still have been destroyed by the controlled explosion and, therefore, that the cave should still be there. He just hoped the console hadn't exploded yet.

It was a short walk to the bomb site, but Joe could see no evidence that the bomb had been discovered yet. This was strange, as it was now the day after he had originally found Max's cave.

"What's happened to the unexploded bomb?" he asked a passing dog walker.

"Bomb? I have no idea what you're talking about," came the reply.

Joe frowned in confusion. "I thought somebody had found an unexploded World War II bomb here. They needed to make the area safe."

The dog walker looked baffled. "What are you talking about? Is this some silly game? What on Verissium is World War II?"

***

By now Joe was feeling incredibly scared and upset. If there was no way to get back into Max's cave, it would be impossible to fix things. He was also incredibly confused at this weird timeline he'd found himself in. If there had been no World War II, that would mean that millions of lives had been saved – which, obviously, was a good thing. So did it even need fixing? He supposed he could cope with the occasional pterodactyl attack, and the mantra was a small price to pay for the millions of lives that had been spared the horrors of that war.

It had only just occurred to him that he hadn't looked at the internet since he'd returned, so he reached into his pocket for his smartphone. It wasn't there. He didn't use it that much, but it was always in his bag. *It must be at home,* he thought.

Joe arrived back home approximately ten minutes later and headed straight upstairs. Milo followed, joining Joe in his bedroom. There was still no sign of his smartphone. So, he logged onto his computer and tried to find the desktop link to his social media page.

"That's odd," he said to Milo. It wasn't there. He couldn't find any way to access the internet either.

He heard a door close downstairs and then a voice shouted out, "It's only me!" It was his mum.

Joe went back downstairs. "I'll make you a cup of tea," he said, putting the kettle on.

"That's so lovely," his mum replied, "thanks."

Joe had so many questions, but he didn't want his mum thinking he'd gone crazy. "Is the broadband working?" he asked casually. "I can't seem to get on the internet."

His mum looked at him with an expression of bemusement. "What's the internet?"

Joe was horrified. How was he going to find the Robinsons without the internet? He didn't even know the professor's first name!

"What's the internet?" asked his mum again.

"It's nothing, Mum," he replied. "I was just messing about."

Joe decided he was going to have to go old school and use books to learn more about the timeline he was stuck in. "I'm going to the library," he told his mum, hoping that libraries were still a thing.

"What, now?" asked his mum.

"Yes, is that a problem?"

Joe's mum stared at him, a look of confusion and anger battling across her features. "Of course it's a problem ¬– it's almost five o clock."

Joe glanced out of the window. It was dark outside, but this had never been a problem before. So what had changed? Joe knew he had to ask what she meant but he didn't want to come across any crazier than he already had.

He was just about to ask when a loud siren sounded. This was followed by what Joe assumed was a pre-recorded message.

"The curfew has started. It is a criminal offence for any citizen to be outside of their home between now and six o'clock tomorrow morning."

"We put our faith in the order of Verissimus."

It was the same voice that had delivered the mantra earlier in the day. Joe was desperate to find out what was going on, as well as why everyone seemed so comfortable with it.

"Can I call Dad please?" asked Joe.

"You know that we're only allowed to call the rig on Sundays," replied his mum.

Joe was disappointed, but relieved that nothing bad seemed to have happened to his dad.

After dinner, Joe went back up to his bedroom and, after browsing his bookshelf, he noticed he had an encyclopaedia. This was bound to give him some information, surely?

This particular book included a history of the world from AD 143 – there was no mention of any earlier history. It explained that all the countries in the world are united under the leadership of the Order of Verissimus. It also said that, apart from a small number of attempted revolts, there had been global peace since the time of the Roman Empire. The Roman Empire had evolved into the Order of Verissimus. The whole world celebrated this by repeating a mantra on all five weekdays.

The encyclopaedia also included a whole section about the centuries-old struggle to control the 'birds', and how it had been important to introduce a night-time curfew, as this was when they were most active. That explains the announcement, he thought.

Joe was just about to close the book and go to sleep when he noticed something strange: there was a passage that referred to a global language. He read on and soon realised that the global language was Latin.

But everyone here has been speaking English, he thought.

Slowly, the truth dawned on him.

"I've still got the Lingua worm in my ear!" he said aloud.

This was when he really started to panic. Max had told them all that the worm would hatch and grow before eventually crawling back out of the ear. This would take approximately three weeks, after which they would no longer be able to understand any foreign languages.

Joe spoke aloud again. "In two weeks' time… I won't be able to understand or speak to anybody!"

He knew that now, more than ever, he had to find the Robinsons. They would have been home for a year already and it would be another two years before the professor would complete his portable time machine. They would no longer have translator worms and would probably be hiding somewhere.

Yawning, Joe decided to go to sleep. He needed to rest before trying to find the Robinsons the next day.

Just as he was about to close the encyclopaedia, however, he noticed an image on one of the pages about the medieval times. The image showed that there had still been knights in the medieval times and that they had attempted to overthrow the Order of Verissimus. As he studied the picture more closely, his heart raced and his whole body began to tremble.

The image showed that the armed forces leader of the Order of Verissimus in the medieval period was none other than Dardan.

***

104

The next morning, Joe had another look through the encyclopaedia. There were no other images of Dardan or any mentions of his name anywhere in the book. It was as if he had disappeared during the Middle Ages.

As Joe had no idea how he was going to find the Robinson family, he thought it would be best if he went to school. At least this would stop him from drawing any unwanted attention to himself.

So, after breakfast, he set off on his usual route to school. He was conscious of the pterodactyl risk, but he couldn't see anything unusual in the sky.

"Hello mate."

Joe turned around to see Mo approaching him.

Together, the two friends continued the short walk to school. Joe really wanted to tell Mo everything, but thought it would be best if he didn't. What if Mo didn't believe him?

When they arrived at school they headed straight to their form group. At least Joe knew what to expect now, and he quickly stood up and joined in when the mantra started.

For the rest of the day, Joe found his newly acquired knowledge to be extremely useful. If he could just learn Latin, then he could possibly get used to this timeline.

The day passed by without any 'bird' attacks and, before long, school was over.

Joe and Mohammed were walking home when a convoy of ten army vehicles passed by.

"They must be searching for traitors," said Mo.

"I guess so," replied Joe, not wanting to show his ignorance again. He was, however, starting to feel incredibly anxious. What had Mo meant by that? Why was it so normal to be 'searching for traitors'?

"Shall we go to the Henge at the weekend?" asked Mo. "Saturday?"

"Where?" replied Joe.

"What do you mean, where?" snapped a frustrated Mo. "Are you being stupid on purpose? Stonehenge."

Joe realised that Stonehenge was, clearly, still close by. That meant that Dardan's cave should be easy to find.

"Yeah, sounds good."

Joe went home, fed Milo, and then looked for any books or leaflets he could find on Stonehenge. It didn't take long; there was an information leaflet in the living room.

The leaflet explained that Stonehenge had mysteriously moved from its original location in Salisbury to its current location just outside Highcross in the year AD 143. It stated that the power of the original Verissimus came from the mystical stones, and it was now a very important historical landmark. The stones were surrounded by the 'Henge', an adrenalin-pumping theme park that had opened during Roman times. It was the oldest and most popular tourist location in the world, having grown from a small circus into an enormous theme park.

How very clever, thought Joe. *They've created a tourist attraction on the site of Dardan's cave. It will always be busy and well-guarded.*

Joe was feeling better now. He could cope with a few more days here and was confident that – despite the guards – he would be able to sneak into Dardan's cave on Saturday.

He smiled as he heard his mum come home from work. "Hi mum!" he shouted.

"Hi love," replied his mum.

Joe headed downstairs just in time to hear the curfew siren sound.

Roll on Saturday, he thought.

Chapter 10

On Saturday morning, Mo arrived at the Jackson house at 10am on the dot and rang the doorbell. Joe's mum answered the door.

"Hi Mrs Jackson," said Mo.

"Hello Mohammed. It's lovely to see you. Come in."

Mo entered the house and sat down in the living room to wait for Joe. He didn't have to wait long.

"Alright mate," said Joe as he entered the living room.

"Alright," replied Mo.

Joe had managed to get through the rest of the week without drawing any attention to himself. His encyclopaedia had given him enough information to have a decent understanding of this strange world, and hopefully today was the day he could start to fix things.

Mrs Jackson had agreed to drive Joe and Mo to the Henge, and then pick them up later so they would be home before curfew.

It was a short journey to the theme park and Joe could hardly contain his excitement, though he knew he'd have to pretend he'd been there before.

The entrance to the theme park was unbelievable. There was an enormous gate, which was flanked by actors dressed as Roman legionaries. As they arrived at the main gate, Joe began to realise it might be more difficult than he'd originally thought to sneak into Dardan's cave.

"Here we are," said Mrs Jackson. "I'll meet you back here at 4 o'clock."

"Thanks, Mrs Jackson," replied Mo.

Joe got out of the car and looked ahead, totally in awe of the scene that greeted him.

"Goodbye Joe," said Mrs Jackson.

"Oh yeah. Thanks, Mum. See you later," replied Joe absentmindedly.

After purchasing their tickets, an excited Joe and Mo headed towards the entrance turnstiles and joined the queue.

"I hope the Silver Sphere ride is working this time," said Mo.

"Silver Sphere?!" Joe exclaimed with surprise.

"Yes," replied Mo. "Remember? It wasn't working last time."

Joe nodded in agreement.

As they approached the front of the queue Joe noticed that the people dressed as Roman legionaries were actually soldiers. *This is so strange,* he thought.

Inside though, it was amazing. It was so much better than any theme park Joe had been to before. It was full of people in the most amazing costumes, it had the highest roller coasters he'd ever seen, and Stonehenge was located right in the centre of the park.

"Let's go straight to the Silver Sphere," suggested Mo.

Joe thought this was a great idea; looking at his site map, he could see this would involve walking across the park, meaning he should be able to see where the entrance to the cave was.

As they walked across the park and got closer to Stonehenge, Joe realised that he couldn't see the entrance to the cave anywhere. It had been on the same level as Stonehenge during AD 143, so surely it should still be on the same level now?

It must be hidden, he thought. *How am I going to get in?*

After a short walk, Joe and Mo arrived at the Silver Sphere. It looked identical to the real Silver Sphere that Joe had travelled in, only it was much bigger. There wasn't much of a queue and, before long, they were able to enter the ride.

Joe sat down in an identical copy of the real time machine he'd travelled back to the Cretaceous period in. There were enough seats for a hundred people and, once it was full, the door closed. The lights went out and, a few moments later, the sphere started to spin. A monitor appeared at the front of the ride and images of different time periods started to appear on the screen as the ride spun faster and faster. In fact, it was the fastest ride Joe had ever experienced, and it did feel very much like the real thing.

"That was amazing!" exclaimed Mo once it was over.

They exited the ride and started wandering around the park. Joe was starting to feel anxious.

Was he going to be stuck here forever? In a world that spoke a language he didn't understand? He desperately needed Max's help.

"Let's get some lunch," suggested Mo.

Joe wasn't particularly hungry but he decided to go along with Mo's idea. So, they went into a fast-food restaurant and Joe sat down while Mo went to the counter to order the food.

Joe was so busy thinking about how he was going to find the cave that he didn't even notice when somebody else sat down at the table.

"Hi Joe."

Joe looked up and nearly let out a scream of joy.

It was Lily!

***

"It's so good to see you!" exclaimed Joe.

Lily smiled and nodded.

Joe was finding it hard to keep up with the ages of the Robinson family. When they had first met in the Cretaceous period Lily was 13 years old. The last time he saw her she was 16. Now she must be around 14. *Time travel is so confusing,* he thought.

"How have you been? Where is the rest of your family?" asked Joe, still amazed and delighted to see her.

Lily seemed reluctant to speak. Instead of talking, she picked up a napkin and started writing. She then handed the napkin to Joe.

I can't speak too much. I don't speak Latin. It would draw far too much attention to me.

Remembering that he still had a Lingua worm in his ear, Joe nodded in agreement. He continued to read the note.

Mum, Dad, and Patrick are here in the park. Meet us at the sky looper ride in ten minutes. Don't bring your friend.

Joe looked around at Mo, who was just about to be served at the counter. When he turned back, Lily was gone.

Mo arrived at the table with the food only to find that Joe had disappeared. Feeling a little annoyed, he sat down and started to eat. He must have gone to the toilet, he thought.

Meanwhile, Joe was looking at his map of the park and walking at speed towards the sky looper ride. He felt bad about leaving Mo behind in the restaurant, but meeting up with the Robinsons was far more important right now.

After a short walk, he arrived at the sky looper ride and immediately saw Lily waiting for him. She pointed towards an unguarded door at the side of the ride before walking through it. Joe was quick to follow.

"How are you, Joe?" asked the professor.

The whole Robinson family was standing directly in front of Joe. He couldn't control his emotions; his eyes started to water as he said, "I can't believe you're here!"

The professor explained that they'd been back for a year. "The weirdest thing," he told Joe, "is the lack of birds – real birds, I mean. Have you noticed that there aren't any?"

Joe started to think. The professor was right. There were no birds.

"That's why the pterodactyls are referred to as birds," the professor explained. "They are the only ones left. We've guessed that they caused the extinction of the other birds centuries ago."

"Well… the pterodactyls were brought to the Roman times by you," said Joe.

"What do you mean?" asked the professor, frowning.

Joe explained that a future version of the family had used four pterodactyls to stage a rescue. It hadn't worked and the pterodactyls had escaped.

Upon hearing this, the Robinsons were horrified.

"I'm sorry I told you," sighed Joe.

"Don't worry; we're pleased that you did. We're going to fix this," replied Mrs Robinson.

The Robinsons had initially tried to settle into this new timeline, she told Joe, but this became impossible when their Lingua worms crawled out. From that moment on they were no longer able to mix with others. They had been lucky when entering the park as nobody had asked any questions.

"We've been hiding ever since," Mrs Robinson concluded. "We knew when you'd be returning, and we knew we needed to meet you and get you home. Which is exactly what we did."

"You did?" Joe asked. He tried to recall his arrival in this timeline, but could only remember waking up at home the following morning.

"You arrived here at the theme park. We knew we had to meet you to stop you being captured," explained the professor. "We managed to sneak in and were here just in time for your arrival. You were very upset and confused, but we managed to get you out of the park and get you home."

"I can't remember any of that," admitted Joe.

"I'm sure it will come back to you," the professor told him. "The important thing is that we are all back together. And we know where the entrance to the cave is."

Joe smiled. "Really?"

"Yes," replied the professor. He went on to explain that the entrance to the cave was through a corridor that could be accessed by the room they were standing in.

This worried Joe. "But why are there no guards here? Is this a trap?"

"Definitely not," said the professor. "We've been here lots of times and nobody has ever tried to stop us. We've concluded that the cave is not guarded because it is impossible to enter."

"What?" replied Joe, his heart sinking. "What do you mean, impossible?"

"Come and see," said the professor.

They all walked down a long, dark corridor before arriving at what looked like the entrance to Dardan's cave. It was completely covered by a huge boulder, and there was a message engraved into the rock.

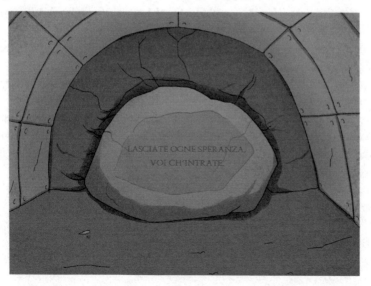

Patrick looked at the engraving and read the words out loud. *"Lasciate ogne Speranza, voi ch'intrate."*

"As we can't read Latin, we've struggled to translate it," said Lily. She looked at Joe. "You'll be able to read it, though. What does it say?"

Joe looked at the phrase that was engraved in the rock and felt his heart sink once again. Slowly, he read the phrase out loud to the others. "Abandon all hope, ye who enter here."

***

Suddenly, they heard the sound of footsteps coming down the corridor.

"Listen… someone's coming. I knew it was a trap!" whispered Joe.

The footsteps were getting closer and there was nowhere to hide.

Professor Robinson stood in front of the group. It was now just about possible to see the silhouette of a person approaching.

"Who's there?" mumbled the professor.

"Veniae?[5]*"* came the reply.

Joe immediately recognised the voice. "Mo, is that you?"

"Of course it's me!" replied Mo. "I followed you here. Who are these people and why are they speaking in a such a weird way?"

"These are my friends and they are speaking English." Joe sighed. "Look, Mo… I need to tell you the truth."

So, Joe told the whole story to Mo. He knew it sounded crazy, but it was a relief for Joe to have shared it with his best friend.

It was obvious, however, that Mo was having a hard time believing what Joe was telling him. This timeline might have seemed unreal to Joe and the Robinsons, but to everybody else it was completely normal.

"Is this for real?" asked a puzzled Mo. "These people can't speak Latin?"

"Yes, it's for real, and we need to put things back to the way they used to be," replied Joe.

Mo looked confused. "But you've just said that in the other

5. Pardon in Latin

timeline there were global wars. Why is that better than here?"

Joe had to admit that he'd been thinking about this very subject, and he decided to ask the professor the same question.

"Have you seen an aeroplane since you arrived here?" asked the professor.

Joe thought about it for a second. "No, I haven't.'

"Most of the things that are familiar to us no longer exist," he explained.

"Such as?" asked Joe.

"The internet, planes, helicopters, high-speed rail, and most of the medicines that we take for granted. Penicillin, for instance, has not been discovered in this timeline."

"Why?" asked Joe.

"As you know, in this timeline, manned flight was discovered in the Roman times, so there was no need for the Wright Brothers to invent the aeroplane. Flight is restricted to the Order of Verissimus and its army. I imagine that the other things were not invented or discovered because the people that were responsible for them were never born."

"Not born?" asked a surprised Joe.

The professor nodded. "We didn't want to give you too much information; it's very upsetting. Since the Roman times, people 'disappearing' has become normal. The population of the planet is much smaller than we remember. As a result, many of the great people in our timeline were never even born."

"Is it the pterodactyls?" asked Joe.

"We think so," replied Mrs Robinson.

Mo was listening to the translation being provided by Joe when it occurred to him that every family he knew (including his own) had a high number of missing people. "I believe you," he said to Joe. "What do we need to do?"

A relieved Joe introduced Mo to the Robinson family. He needed to act as a translator so that everyone could understand what was being said, but they did their best to greet each other.

"We need to get through this boulder," said the professor, pointing at the large rock.

The group looked around for anything that might help them break or move the boulder, but after several minutes they'd found nothing.

"There must be a way in," said Patrick. "Why does this corridor even exist if nobody uses this cave?"

The group pondered for a moment, before realising that time was running out. The park would be closing soon, and the chances of capture would be much higher.

"We got lucky on the night we arrived, and the night we rescued you," explained a concerned professor, "but our luck will run out if your mum reports you missing; they'll search the whole park for you. Let's try again tomorrow. Will your mum let you come back?"

Joe said that he thought it would be fine.

They'd all just started walking back up the corridor when they heard a loud siren.

"Is that a pterodactyl alert?" asked Joe.

"No," replied the professor. "It's a fire alarm. They'll be evacuating the park."

"A fire alarm?" Joe repeated, sounding worried.

The group reached the end of the corridor and found themselves back at the door they'd entered through a short time ago. They quickly exited the room and noticed that the park was, indeed, deserted.

"What now?" asked Joe.

Before anybody could answer, a whooshing sound was heard coming from above. They all looked up to see a small army gliding towards them.

"Nice to see you!" boomed a voice from the sky. "We've been waiting centuries for this day!"

Joe and the Robinsons were gripped with fear. It was Verissimus.

Chapter 11

Joe couldn't believe what was happening and who he was seeing. His mind was awash with questions. How could Verissimus still be alive? Had he travelled through time as well? How did they know where to find him – and the Robinsons?

"Thank you for your service, professor," said Verissimus.

"It was an honour, sir," replied the professor.

Joe snapped his head around to look at the professor. What was going on?

Lily, Patrick, and Mrs Robinson didn't understand what was happening either – mainly because the professor was speaking to Verissimus in Latin.

With the benefit of the Lingua worm, Joe knew only too well that the professor had betrayed them. "How could you?" he shouted.

"Did you honestly think the cave wouldn't be guarded?" laughed Verissimus. "The good professor here has been helping me draw you all into a trap."

By now Lily, Patrick, and Mrs Robinson had got the gist of what was happening, and they all looked devastated.

"Dad, why?" cried Patrick.

The professor didn't answer. Instead, he opened the door and walked back down the corridor that led to Dardan's cave.

Mo was feeling even more confused than he had been just a short while ago. He couldn't stop thinking about all the people that had mysteriously disappeared over the years. Was he next?

Verissimus and his army glided down to the ground, approaching Joe, Mo, and the remaining members of the Robinson family. They quickly took them prisoner.

"You should have just lived your life here," said Verissimus, "but you wanted to get back into the cave. Well, I'm here to make your dream come true!"

They all headed back down the corridor and into the cave. By the time they arrived, the professor was nowhere to be seen and the boulder was gone. Joe realised that this wasn't exactly an ideal situation, but at least they were going to get back to the cave.

The passages in the cave system were very familiar to Joe and the Robinsons; the inside of the cave had not changed much in the last 1849 years.

As they continued walking towards the central cavern, Verissimus announced, "You are just in time to see our plan come to fruition!"

Joe was now feeling utterly confused. *What plan?* he thought. *You've already taken over the world.*

Mo, meanwhile, was still trying to figure out what on Verissium was going on. He thought he must be dreaming.

As they approached the central cavern, Joe caught a glimpse of something moving in the darkness. *What was that?* he thought.

The central cavern looked the same as it had all those centuries ago, and Joe noticed that the portal button was still blinking. Was that how Verissimus had been able to get here? He couldn't see any sign of Max or Dardan.

"We aren't stopping here," said Verissimus.

Suddenly, the army turned into a passage to the left of the central cavern, taking the prisoners along with them.

"Do you remember what the engraving on the boulder said?" asked Verissimus.

The Robinsons were unable to understand what was being said, but Joe and Mo could clearly remember.

"*Lasciate ogne Speranza, voi ch'intrate,*" said Mo.

"Well done, young man," responded Verissimus. "Joe, would you like to remind the lovely Robinson family of the translation?"

"Abandon all hope, ye who enter here," said Joe, his voice devoid of emotion.

"Yes," replied Verissimus. "Now, why do you think we might need a warning like that?"

Joe shrugged.

"Well," said Verissimus, "we have been looking after some very special creatures here in the cave. They do get very hungry, though. They have an insatiable appetite for human meat, so we have to make sure that we occasionally let them roam free."

The army and their prisoners stopped at the edge of a large hole.

"Don't worry," said Verissimus. "There's a nice slope down to the bottom. We don't want the fall to kill you."

Before they even knew what was happening, the army pushed the prisoners down into the hole. They found themselves sliding down a steep slope, which quickly took them to the bottom of the hole.

"Is everybody okay?" asked Joe, before looking around.

Suddenly, he recoiled in horror. The others had noticed as well.

I think I know where all the missing people have gone, thought a panicked Joe.

Mo gulped.

The hole was full of hundreds of sleeping pterodactyls.

***

The pterodactyl pit was enormous; the light emanating from the passages above was enough to illuminate the vast cavern and show just how many pterodactyls were living there.

"Don't make a sound," whispered Joe.

"Don't worry. I wasn't going to," replied Mo, also in a whisper.

Mrs Robinson beckoned the others towards her. "We need to find a way out," she said in a hushed tone. "Look around for a way out – but do it quietly."

The group moved carefully and silently around the pit, studying every crack and crevice, but there didn't seem to be any way to get out. The slope was too steep to climb, and there didn't seem to be any other passages leading out of the pit.

"We're t-trapped!" stuttered a panicked Mo. "I wish I hadn't followed you through that door."

Joe, who was the only person who could understand what Mo was saying, replied, "Don't worry, mate. I've been in worse situations recently." He said it in a reassuring manner, but Mo wasn't convinced.

It was then that Patrick noticed a kind of glistening directly ahead of him. Carefully and cautiously, he approached it. "It looks like a magnifying glass," he pondered out loud.

This made Joe look up. "Say that again!"

"It's a magnifying glass," repeated Patrick, frowning in confusion.

Joe walked carefully over to the spot where Patrick was standing. "It's a trekker. How did it get here?" he asked rhetorically.

"A what?" said Patrick.

"It's how the people from Max's planet travel around," Joe replied, picking up the trekker and studying it.

Mrs Robinson approached Joe. "How does it work?"

"I don't know," Joe admitted, sighing.

All of a sudden, a loud squawk echoed around the pit – the pterodactyls were waking up.

"We haven't got long," hissed a frightened Lily. "We need to figure out how this thing works *now*!"

As Joe continued examining the magnifying glass, he noticed a dial on the side of the handle. There was also a small crack in the glass itself. He desperately tried to remember what Max had done when they'd visited the pyramids. As he moved the dial, he noticed that an image of the central cavern appeared in the glass.

Meanwhile, the sounds of the waking pterodactyls were getting louder and louder.

"Hurry!" shouted Mo.

Joe pressed a button on the other side of the handle and a portal appeared in front of them. "Follow me!" he ordered as he walked through.

The others followed, being met with a bright flash of light as they passed through the portal.

Moments later, the group found themselves in a seemingly deserted central cavern. It was so empty it felt eerie.

"Have we travelled in time?" asked Lily.

"No," said Joe. "We're still in the same time."

As the group approached the main console, they all noticed the flashing portal light.

"That means it's operational," said Joe, feeling relieved – though what he really wanted to do was find Max. The last time he'd been in this cave, Max had been turned into stone. *Surely we can reverse it*, thought Joe.

The rest of the group were standing at the main console when an alarm suddenly started ringing out.

"I didn't touch anything!" Patrick shouted.

Joe ran over to the main console to join the others. As well as the alarm, all of the lights on the console were flashing. Then, just moments later, the cave started to vibrate.

"It's a portal!" said Mrs Robinson, just as the portal appeared in the centre of the cavern.

The group looked on as, slowly, a figure came into view. A whooshing sound accompanied this appearance, and in an instant the cavern was filled with gliding soldiers.

"How did you escape?!" screamed Verissimus.

The figure was getting clearer and clearer as a loud howl echoed around the cavern.

It was now obvious who was coming through the portal.

It was Dardan.

As the portal closed, the alarm stopped ringing and the lights stopped flashing. The only light still blinking was on the portal button.

"How is it we keep meeting?" Dardan asked, looking at Joe and the Robinsons before resting his gaze on Mo. "And I see you've managed to get a new friend mixed up in your mess as well."

"Where's my dad?!" shouted Lily.

"You mean my loyal servant?" replied Dardan. "Don't worry; he is quite safe. He is looking after one of my projects in the distant past. I'm afraid you won't be seeing him again."

The Robinsons all started to cry. They simply couldn't believe that the professor was working for Dardan.

Patrick, however, suddenly had a thought. *They must be controlling Dad's mind!* "We need to go back to the Middle Ages to rescue him," he whispered to his mum.

"Where's Max?" Joe asked Dardan.

"Ah, Maxelon. He's long gone," Dardan replied, sighing. "I wanted to keep him on display, but unfortunately he was destroyed hundreds of years ago – smashed into thousands of pieces." He shook his head. "Anyhow, you are just in time to see the final stages of my plan for global domination. I've decided that I preferred the prehistoric times; humans are vermin. So, I think it's time to give the dinosaurs their planet back." He looked at Verissimus. "Thank you for your help, but I need to take my planet back now."

All of a sudden, a squawking sound could be heard floating down one of the passages. Within seconds the pterodactyls appeared and immediately started to devour the army of Verissimus. Joe, Mo, and the Robinsons looked on in horror. Before long, there were no soldiers left.

"Your turn," said Dardan as a pterodactyl knocked Verissimus off his glider.

When he hit the ground, he exploded into several pieces.

"He was a robot!" shouted Joe, his mouth hanging open.

"Of course," said Dardan. "Did you think he was over 1800

years old?" He approached the main console again and pressed the blinking button. The cave started to vibrate and, once again, a portal opened in the centre of the cavern.

Through the portal rushed the sound of a thousand roars.

"Look at the monitor," Dardan instructed.

They all looked up at the monitor above the main console, which was now revealing a terrifying sight. There were portals opening all over the world.

"It has taken all this time for the cave to build up enough power from Stonehenge," explained Dardan, "but finally, it is ready!"

Now, the monitor showed hundreds of dinosaurs passing through the portals.

"Everyone will be killed!" shouted Mrs Robinson, aghast.

"There's always room for humans in my new world. Any survivors will be my slaves," replied Dardan casually as he approached the portal in the centre of the cavern.

The group looked on in horror as thousands of dinosaurs poured out of the portal, running into the passages and out into the closed theme park beyond.

While Dardan was distracted in the centre of the cavern, Patrick walked up to the main console. He remembered how to open a portal and was able to find the previous time zones that had been visited using this console. He pushed the blinking portal button and waited.

By now the final dinosaur had come through the portal, which then disappeared in a flash.

Once again, Dardan approached the main console.

"You are welcome to watch what happens on the monitor," he told the others. "I can't save you from the dinosaurs, though." He shrugged. "Enjoy it while you can."

Joe was starting to feel sick. *What's going to happen to my mum and dad?* he thought desperately.

Patrick walked towards the centre of the cavern and beckoned the others to join him. As they did, the cave started vibrating again.

"What have you done?!" shouted Dardan, whipping his head around to glare at Patrick just as another portal appeared.

"Run!" shouted Patrick.

As fast as they could, the group ran into the portal, leaving Dardan alone in his cave.

*　*　*

There was a bright flash of light and then the group emerged in the middle of a forest.

"When are we?" asked Joe.

Patrick looked around. "The console had been previously set to the year AD 462. I think this is where my dad is," he explained.

Mo took in his surroundings, wide-eyed. He had no idea what was going on and he still couldn't understand a thing the Robinsons were saying.

"Where are we?" he asked Joe.

Joe put a comforting hand on his friend's arm, before replying, "The Middle Ages."

Part 5: The Middle Ages

Chapter 12

"Where's the cave?" asked Mo. "Why are we in a field?"

Joe didn't really understand everything that had happened, but he'd done enough time travelling by now to know that the cave would be close by. "It will be around here somewhere," he replied.

Patrick had already started looking around for the entrance to the cave. They needed to rescue his dad and then figure out a way to put things back to normal.

Mrs Robinson was still very distressed about what they'd left behind, back in 2022. "Those poor people," she sighed, "with all those dinosaurs!"

"Don't worry, Mum," said Lily, smiling encouragingly. "It hasn't happened yet. We can fix it."

Patrick had been continuing his search for the cave, and it didn't take long before he found an enormous clue. "It's Stonehenge!" he shouted.

The rest of the group ran over to meet him and, sure enough, directly in front of Stonehenge was the entrance to the cave.

"This is risky," Joe told the rest of the group. "We always get caught whenever we enter this cave. We need to have a very quick look for the professor and then figure out how to fix the future. And we need to be careful."

Agreeing with Joe, the group cautiously entered the cave and started walking nervously towards the central cavern. By now, they all knew the passages in this cave like the backs of their hands, and it didn't take long to get to their destination.

The cave was empty. The main console had no blinking lights and showed no signs of life. It definitely looked like it was deserted.

Suddenly, Joe remembered something he'd read in his book. "Dardan lives on the surface in the Middle Ages!" he exclaimed. "I saw it in my encyclopaedia."

Whilst the rest of the group looked around the cave, searching for clues to help them find the professor, Patrick walked up to the main console. He still remembered how to work it but it didn't seem to have any power at all.

It's only been a few hundred years since the Roman times, he thought. *Maybe it hasn't obtained enough power from Stonehenge yet.*

Mo was starting to feel a little more relaxed, and the emptiness of the cave was also making him feel a little braver. He approached a statue in one corner of the cave. It looked like a teenager.

It's so realistic, he thought, before shouting out, "Look at this!"

The Robinsons heard this as "*Vide hoc!*" but Joe was on hand to translate.

As everyone approached the realistic-looking statue, the Robinsons immediately began to smile.

Joe stared at the statue and felt a sense of hope fill his body as his eyes started watering.

"What's the matter?" asked a – still very confused – Mo.

"It's Max," replied Joe, smiling widely.

***

Joe ran over to the main console. "We have to figure out how to free him. Come on, Patrick – I need your help!"

Patrick looked at the console and its vast array of buttons. "I don't know where to start," he said. "Dad and I only figured out how to open a portal."

Joe thought for a moment before asking Patrick, "Which buttons didn't you and your dad use when you both figured out how to use the console?"

Patrick noticed a button that he was confident had nothing to do with time travel. "We didn't use this one," he said, pointing at it.

"Are you sure?" asked Joe.

"Positive."

Slowly and cautiously, Joe pressed the button.

The console immediately came to life, and the same strip of light that they'd seen back in the Roman times shone out from the dashboard. This beam of light moved immediately in the direction of Max and, as the light touched the 'statue', the rock started breaking off. Within seconds, the statue was no more.

It had been replaced by a fully living, fully breathing, Max.

"Thank you!" gasped Max. "How long was I stuck like that?"

Joe ran over to him and gave him a hug. "It's... been a while," he replied.

The group provided Max with an explanation of everything that had happened whilst he'd been out of action. Max soon realised that there were language difficulties within the group and pulled out a handful of Lingua worm eggs from his pocket.

"You want me to put that in my ear?" asked Mo, raising his eyebrows.

"Yes," replied Max. "You'll be able to understand what the Robinsons are saying."

Reluctantly, Mo put the egg in his ear. "Say something please," he said to Lily.

"Hi Mo," said Lily.

Mo smiled. He could finally understand English.

"We need to get out of here and find the professor," said Max. "I promise we'll be able to fix everything."

Joe took the trekker out of his pocket. "Let's use this," he said. "We found it in a pit in 2022. I'm not sure how it got there…"

Max took the trekker from Joe, and when he held it out he saw that a destination had already been programmed into it. He pressed the button on the handle and the image of a small village appeared on the glass just as a portal appeared in front of the group.

They all entered, and – with a flash of light – they found themselves standing in a medieval town.

***

"How far have we travelled?" asked Joe.

"Not far," replied Max. "This trekker is old; it hasn't got that much power left. I would think that we are less than ten miles from the cave."

The village appeared to be traditionally medieval; it looked just like the pictures and films of medieval places that Joe, Mo, and the Robinsons had seen.

"We need to find some different clothes," suggested Max as he looked at what they were all wearing. "We seemed very out of place in the Roman times. We'll stand out too much dressed like this."

The others agreed as they glanced at their surroundings. The village was quiet but it didn't seem to be deserted.

"It's early," observed Joe. "Everybody must be asleep."

The group looked around for some clothes they could borrow. Fortunately, there were plenty of clothes that had been hung up to dry on nearby washing lines.

"We'll return these later," said Max, taking down some tunics and trousers.

They quickly changed – leaving their own clothes safely hidden under a small bridge – and then decided to head further into the village, just as the sound of a crowing cockerel reached their ears.

"This is amazing!" exclaimed a now thoroughly excited Mo. "I can't believe I'm here!" He was taking in every single sight with a kind of wide-eyed wonder.

"It doesn't smell very nice though," said Lily, with a sick feeling in her mouth. The streets were full of rubbish. There were also a lot of farm animals seemingly living wild in the town.

"Watch your step!" warned Patrick, just as Lily stood in something quite disgusting.

"Gross!" she screeched.

They were still making their way into the centre of the village when they all noticed something very interesting: there were pictures of Verissimus all over the walls. These pictures, however, had been covered in graffiti and extremely rude language.

Joe recalled what he'd read in his encyclopaedia. "There were attempted revolts against the Order of Verissimus in the Middle

Ages," he informed his friends. "The people in this place must be involved in one of those revolts."

Max looked at one of the posters. "We are definitely in the right place. We should be able to find some friends here."

"What about my husband?" asked Mrs Robinson.

"We'll find him," Max promised her as he walked towards a small tavern that was just opening its doors for the day. "Let's go in here."

The group headed in and sat down.

"What will we be able to buy in a medieval cafe?" asked Mrs Robinson. "We don't have any money."

Max explained that they weren't there to buy food; they were there to gather information. "This village hates Verissimus; that means they are our friends."

A moment later, a young man walked in and sat down at a table on the other side of the café. He was dressed like a knight.

"I can't believe it," said Joe. "It's a real knight!"

Max got up from the table and walked over to the young knight, before sitting down and starting to talk.

The rest of the group – who were unable to hear what was being said – could only wait in anticipation.

A few minutes later, Max returned to the table. He wasn't alone; the knight had accompanied him.

"This is a friend. He has been fighting the armies of Verissimus for many months now and wants to help us," explained Max.

Joe looked at the knight. "Nice to meet you. I'm Joe."

The knight stared at the unusual group assembled before him. "Nice to meet you all," he said in a deep, booming voice. "My name is Arthur of Camelot."

***

Mo nearly fell out of his chair. "Arthur, King of Camelot?!" he shouted in excitement.

Arthur gave Mo a puzzled look. "I'm not a king," he said. "The ruler of Camelot is a man called The Professor."

The Robinsons exchanged worried glances, understanding that they had to head for Camelot.

"Who is this professor?" asked Mrs Robinson.

"Nobody knows," replied Arthur. "He appeared from nowhere and the Order of Verissimus immediately put him in charge. He runs a very brutal regime. Camelot is now a dangerous place."

"We have to go there," pleaded Patrick.

"*Please*," added Lily.

Max agreed and asked Arthur to guide them.

"Of course," Arthur replied. "We'll take back Camelot first and then the rest of this land as well."

Mo couldn't stop grinning.

"What's up with you?" asked Lily.

"It's King Arthur!" replied Mo, practically bouncing up and down in his chair. "This is the most amazing thing that's ever happened to me. I'm going to enjoy being a time traveller!"

"It's a long way to Camelot," said Arthur, ignoring the puzzling words coming out of Mo's mouth. "We need to leave immediately."

Max agreed and told the rest of the group to get ready for the journey.

"How long will it take?" asked Joe.

"It's a long way," repeated Arthur, "and there will be many dangers. We will have to try to avoid the armies of Verissimus as well as the flocks of birds that hunt in the areas we will be passing through."

Joe had forgotten about the pterodactyls. "Oh yeah, the birds."

The group left the tavern and started on their journey to Camelot, walking without incident until the sun began to go down.

"It will be safer to head into the forest and set up camp," Arthur informed them. "It's not safe to be out at night. The birds are very active in this area after dark."

Nobody was going to disagree with Arthur of Camelot, so they all headed into the forest. Max and Arthur looked for a safe place to set up camp whilst the rest of the group waited patiently under a large oak tree.

Mo was still feeling incredibly excited about the situation he'd found himself in, and he still couldn't believe they were going to Camelot with King Arthur.

Joe, on the other hand, was feeling very confused. "How do you know the legend of King Arthur?" he asked Mo. "In your timeline there was no King Arthur. The Order of Verissimus has been in control of the whole world since the Roman times, right?"

Mo looked at Joe with an expression of bemusement. "Of course there was a King Arthur – he was the King of Camelot! It was once the only place in the world that was not ruled by the Order of Verissimus. It only became part of the Order after King Arthur died of old age and the people of Camelot surrendered. In my timeline, The Professor was not the ruler of Camelot."

Joe and the Robinsons exchanged concerned glances. They were all extremely concerned, as it was now clear that even the timeline Mo came from was changing.

"We need to fix this and put everything back to normal," said Joe.

Mrs Robinson agreed. "We need to recover *our* timeline. That's the correct one."

135

Joe, Lily, and Patrick nodded in agreement.

Mo, however, was not so convinced. He now realised that, as a time traveller, changes to the timeline would not affect him personally. He would stay the same. If the world went back to 'normal', he would be stuck in a country that spoke English, whereas he could only speak Latin. Without the permanent help of a Lingua worm, he wouldn't be able to speak to or understand anyone. It sounded terrible.

He decided to keep these thoughts to himself.

Max and Arthur returned to the rest of the group having found a safe place to camp for the night. Arthur had already lit a fire and the group sat around the flames to keep warm. Earlier, when they were in the tavern, they had thought ahead and taken some bread, so now they were able to have a simple – but much appreciated – meal. After they'd eaten, they lay down on the floor and, due to exhaustion, quickly fell asleep.

A couple of hours later, Joe woke suddenly. Something was approaching.

He looked around but, in the pitch-blackness of the woods, he couldn't see anything. He rubbed his eyes and, slowly, they adjusted to the darkness.

From out of the gloom, he heard a twig break.

"What's that?" asked an also now awake Mo.

"I'm not sure," whispered Joe.

It wasn't long before they could both see what was approaching, and it was a sight that made Joe's blood run cold.

Scrambling to his feet, Joe shouted as loud as he could, "It's a bear!"

***

"Monty!" Arthur shouted excitably as the large brown bear ran towards him.

"Monty?" asked a confused Mo.

"Yes. He's my best friend; we've known each other since he was a cub. He accompanies me on all my adventures. He's been hiding in the woods, where it's safer."

A now wide awake Mrs Robinson looked angrily at Arthur. "You could have warned us!"

"I'm sorry," replied Arthur, rather sheepishly. "I was going to introduce you all to him tomorrow. He must have gotten too excited. We can all go back to sleep; Monty will keep us safe."

As Joe and the group settled back down to go to sleep, they all felt a little safer knowing Monty was watching over them.

Chapter 13

The next morning, Lily and Patrick were the first to wake up. Cautiously, they approached Monty, who was lying down in the middle of the group.

"Hello Monty," said Lily. "My name is Lily, and this is my brother, Patrick."

Monty opened his eyes and looked at the Robinson twins.

"Good morning," added Patrick.

Monty sat up and held out his paws.

"He wants to shake your hands," said Arthur, who'd just woken up.

Lily and Patrick glanced at each other and then back at Monty. They each held out a hand, and Monty reached out and took hold of them in his paws. He then pulled the twins towards him and hugged them both.

"He likes you," said Arthur with a smile.

Lily giggled. She'd never been hugged by a bear before.

Joe and Mo immediately ran over to Monty and held out their hands. After letting Lily and Patrick go, Monty gave them a hug too.

"It's so nice to see them happy. This has been a very strange and upsetting time for us," Mrs Robinson said to Arthur.

"The Order of Verissimus has caused so much heartache," Arthur replied, shaking his head. "When we get to Camelot, we will fix everything once and for all."

"I hope you're right," sighed Mrs Robinson.

Max was standing at the edge of the campsite, watching everything that was going on. He knew he needed to fix this. He was fully aware that the disruption to the timeline had everything to do with him and Dardan but, while he was feeling guilty about that, he also felt positive about the mission ahead.

He shouted at the group, "Let's go! The sooner we arrive in Camelot the sooner we can all get home!"

After breakfast, the group packed up their things and set off on the next stage of their big adventure. By now, Mo and Monty had become very close. They were so close, in fact, that Monty was letting Mo ride him.

"This is amazing!" shouted Mo. "Much better than riding a horse!"

"Does Monty mind?" Mrs Robinson asked Arthur.

"Not at all," he replied, smiling at the sight of Mo and Monty.

"How much further is Camelot?" enquired Joe.

"It's still a very long way," said Arthur. "It would take many days to walk there."

Max, Joe, Mrs Robinson, and the twins suddenly felt much less optimistic.

"Many days?" repeated Lily.

"Yes," replied Arthur. "However, fear not – we are not walking all the way there."

"Stop!" shouted Max.

The group stopped. Mo and Monty, who were ahead of the rest of the group, turned around and came back to join the others.

"Arthur, explain yourself," demanded Max.

Arthur leant against a stump along the side of the road. "I was going to surprise you."

Max was getting angrier. "We've had enough unpleasant surprises recently. Tell us now."

"Did you really think that I walked for days every time I visited other parts of the country?" Arthur asked him. "The Order of Verissimus has very advanced ways of moving around. We are going to use their machine; it's only a couple of hours away."

Despite this development, Max decided that he could still trust Arthur. "Okay," he said eventually, "let's carry on."

They continued their walk for another two hours, during which they didn't see any other people. This hadn't gone unnoticed by the group.

"Where is everyone?" asked Joe.

"People very rarely leave the towns and villages. They fear the birds," Arthur explained.

"But we haven't seen any birds," Patrick pointed out.

"Or any soldiers," added Lily.

"That is unusual," agreed Arthur, "although the soldiers do tend to stay in the towns. I guarantee you will see plenty of them in Camelot. And the birds mainly hunt at night." He pointed to their left. "We need to head into the forest now. That's where the machine is."

The group followed Arthur into the forest and, after a short walk among the trees, they came across a clearing. Max looked at the middle of the clearing in disbelief.

"That's it!" he exclaimed.

Max and Joe immediately recognised the machine. It was an enormous trekker.

***

Max and Joe ran towards the giant trekker, which looked like a huge magnifying glass and was approximately half the size of Joe's house.

"This is enormous!" exclaimed Joe. "They could transport so many people through this. It's no wonder they were able to take over the world. Have you seen one this big before?" he asked Max.

Max studied it carefully. "No, I've never seen one this big before. They don't exist like this on my planet."

The rest of the group joined Max and Joe at the trekker.

"How does it work?" asked Mo.

Arthur walked over to the small console that sat directly under the trekker. "You write the name of your destination here and it appears in the glass. Then we just walk through."

"How many of these things are there?" asked Max.

"There are hundreds," replied Arthur. "It's how the armies of Verissimus move around. This one, though, seems to have been deserted. I've used it many times without being caught, but we need to wait until nightfall to use it. The other machine we're going to use in Camelot is in the centre of the city; we will get caught if we go through during the day."

Whilst most of the group sat down and rested, Max continued to study the giant trekker. He was both confused and concerned about where the technology had come from.

"Did these machines exist in your version of 2022?" he asked Mo.

"Not that I'm aware of," said Mo.

"The timeline seems to be changing every time we travel," pondered Max.

Joe, Mo, Lily, and Patrick were running around with Monty, and – for the first time in days – they were having fun. Before long, the sun started to go down.

"Let's get ready to go," said Arthur.

The group all approached the console and Arthur typed the word 'Camelot' into the keyboard.

Immediately, the enormous trekker started to hum, and an image slowly started appearing in the glass.

"There she is," said Arthur. "The beautiful city of Camelot, capital of the Kingdom of Logres."

Max pulled the group together. "We don't know what to expect when we get to Camelot," he told them, "but no matter what, remember: we have two objectives. One… rescue the professor. Two… find a time portal and fix everything."

With everyone in agreement, the group walked towards the image of Camelot in the glass and then stepped through.

The journey was instantaneous; they walked straight out of the other side of the glass, right into the centre of Camelot. The city was dominated by an enormous castle that took up most of the skyline.

"That's Camelot Castle," said Mo.

"It used to be," Arthur corrected him. "Now it's called Castle Dardan. It is very big with a complicated network of caverns underneath."

Max, Joe, and the Robinsons looked at each other. They were all feeling a strange sense of déjà vu.

Mo frowned. *It was never called Castle Dardan in my history lessons,* he thought.

"Let's go somewhere safe," suggested Arthur. "Fortunately, I have many friends here."

The group moved quickly away from the trekker and into the network of alleyways. Before long, they arrived at a house.

"This house is empty," said Arthur before opening the door. "Come in."

The group entered the house and sat down in the small living quarters.

"Let's get some sleep so that we are ready for our mission tomorrow," suggested Arthur.

The rest of the group were so tired that this seemed like a very good idea. It also felt like a safe place to rest, so they agreed to get some sleep.

Arthur was right: they would need all their energy and strength to face whatever tomorrow brought.

***

The next morning the group were woken with a start by a loud sound coming from outside. It was the sound of trumpets. This was followed by the collective chanting of something much more sinister ¬– and familiar to most of the group.

"We are happy, we are happy, we are happy."
"We are grateful to our beloved leader for his kindness."
"We put our faith in the order of Verissimus."

***

"What is that?" asked Max.

"I'll take this," said Mo, turning to face Max and getting ready to explain. "That is the daily mantra that everybody chants to show their support for the Order of Verissimus. I've been doing it my whole life. I hadn't really thought about how weird it was until I met you lot."

"Do people have a choice?" asked Max.

"No," replied Arthur. "Anyone who is caught not taking part is taken away and never seen again."

Max looked directly at Arthur. "Why didn't we see this in the village where we met? Are the people there not scared of getting caught?"

"Yes, they are scared," replied Arthur. "The armies of Verissimus do sometimes enter that village, but the villagers have managed to stay strong."

Max was starting to get angry. "We must fix this. Dardan and I have caused so many problems here!"

"It's not your fault," said Joe. "You tried to stop him."

The group gathered around Max and reassured him that they did not hold him in any way responsible. This calmed Max down.

By now the mantra had stopped, and Monty had joined the group.

"It's time," said Arthur. "It's only a ten-minute walk to the castle but there will be lots of soldiers along the way. Once we get control of the castle, my friends will be ready to take back Camelot. We just need to figure out how we are going to get into the castle."

"I have a plan," said Joe.

Chapter 14

It was a bright and sunny January morning in Camelot. It was a little bit chilly, but not too cold, and the citizens of the city were just starting their day. The traders were setting up stalls to sell their wares, and shoppers were waiting patiently to purchase their favourite items. There didn't seem to be anything strange about the small group of newcomers walking through the centre of the city and towards the castle.

Arthur was well known within the city and, as such, was wearing a hood on top of his chainmail suit; it was usual for knights to wear hoods and chainmail in Camelot, so he was able to blend in easily. There was also nothing unusual about a young boy riding a bear through the market square. What with all the rumours of wizards about, there had definitely been stranger sights in Camelot.

"Lovely morning, isn't it?" one of the traders asked the group. "Can I interest you in my lovely fruits?"

Approaching the stall, the group looked at the variety of fruits on display.

An English market in the Middle Ages should not be selling such exotic fruits, thought Joe as he picked up a kiwi fruit and ran away.

"Stop! Thief!" shouted the trader.

In an instant, the flying armies of Verissimus descended upon the crime scene.

The market square was now total chaos; all the traders had abandoned their stalls and were chasing the young thief and his accomplices.

Monty and Mo ran down an alleyway, becoming separated from the rest of the group. They tried to find their way back to the market square, but Mo quickly realised that they were completely lost.

They attempted to retrace their steps, but the alleyways were like a maze. Before long, they had even lost sight of the castle.

"Where are we?" Mo asked as he jumped off Monty's back. "We've let everyone else down. How are they going to be able to take control of the castle without your help?" he said to Monty.

Slowly and cautiously, the two friends continued walking deeper into the web of alleys and backstreets.

After a few moments, Monty ran off towards a house at the end of the alley.

"Don't leave me!" pleaded Mo as he chased after the bear.

He ran as fast as he could but by the time he reached the end of the alley, Monty was nowhere to be seen. "How can this be happening?" he whispered to himself, before shouting out, "Monty!"

"Ssshhh!"

"Who was that?" asked Mo, glancing around. He couldn't see anyone.

"It's me," came the reply.

"Who's me?" asked Mo, feeling more confused than ever.

A figure appeared from the house at the end of the alley. Mo couldn't see his face, but he could see that he was wearing dark clothes with a large hood over his head.

"Merlin," came the reply.

***

Meanwhile, back in the market square, the rest of the group were standing in the centre of the market with their hands up.

"We surrender!" shouted Joe.

The leader of the army regiment hovered down to the ground and approached the group. "This is very serious!" he shouted. "The Order of Verissimus does not tolerate theft. You will be taken to the castle. You will answer to The Professor."

Having not realised that they'd lost Mo and Monty, Joe looked at the group and smiled. *It worked,* he thought.

***

"M-Merlin?" stuttered Mo.

"I see you've met my bear."

"Merlin the wizard?" asked Mo.

Merlin raised his eyebrows, looking surprised. "There's no such thing as wizards. Please, come inside."

Cautiously, Mo entered the small house. Monty was waiting for him in the main room. He held out his paw.

"Why did you run off?" Mo asked angrily.

In response, Monty grabbed Mo and embraced him tightly.

"Where have you come from?" Merlin asked him.

Mo had to think carefully about his answer. He didn't think it would be a good idea to tell a stranger – even if he did have the same name as a mythical wizard – that he was a time traveller from the future. He also wasn't sure whether this friendly looking old man was a supporter of Verissimus.

"I've travelled from a long distance to see the wonders of Camelot," said Mo after thinking for a moment.

"With my bear?" responded Merlin. "Do you know Arthur of Camelot?"

Mo wasn't sure how to reply to this. Was it a trap? He looked to Monty for guidance.

In response, the bear stood up on his hind legs, reached for Merlin, and gave him a hug. This instantly reassured Mo.

"Yes, I know Arthur. I have come here with my friends to defeat the Order of Verissimus," he declared, "but I think my friends have been captured and taken to the castle. Arthur is with them."

"A noble cause," replied Merlin, "but how are you going to help your friends?"

"I don't know," admitted Mo.

Merlin gestured for Mo to sit down. "Let me tell you a story."

Merlin explained that he'd been working with Arthur and a group of rebels to overthrow the Order of Verissimus. He explained that Arthur was the rightful ruler of Camelot and the Kingdom of Logres.

"It is his birthright," he finished. "We have been fighting against this evil for most of our lives. It was part of Arthur's plan to bring you here. I'm sorry we didn't tell you, but Monty brought you here intentionally."

"Why?" asked a slightly annoyed Mo.

"We needed to make sure that you and Monty were not captured. You are both needed to help us liberate Camelot," replied Merlin.

"How?" asked Mo, now utterly confused.

"Look outside," Merlin told him.

Mo opened the front door, looked out into the alley, and saw a most amazing sight.

Wow! he thought as he looked upon what must have been at least a hundred knights.

"This is our army," said Merlin. "Now, we just need to wait for a signal."

***

"Where have they gone?!" screamed Dardan.

He approached the main console and frantically attempted to check the destination of the last portal that had been opened. He suspected that they'd gone back to the Middle Ages as that was the last destination saved in the console memory.

"What is wrong with this thing?" he shouted, pressing buttons and getting no response.

Desperately, he started looking for the problem. His monitors were showing that all the portals that had been releasing dinosaurs into the 21st century had now closed, though he could also see that thousands of dinosaurs had indeed passed through the portals before they'd closed.

What have they done? he wondered. *They've ruined my plan!*

"Never mind," he said to himself, after taking a deep breath. "There are more than enough dinosaurs to take back this miserable planet. Most of the humans will soon be gone, and then I will call upon the rest of the Wolfian race to destroy the dinosaurs and colonise Earth."

He let out a loud howl before noticing that the main console was now not responding at all. The portal light had stopped blinking. Staring at the static light, Dardan realised what had happened.

He realised that someone (Max, Joe, or Patrick) had removed the portal energiser chip. He was trapped in 2022.

"I'm stuck here. I can't travel in time or contact my Wolfian compatriots!" he shouted out into the cavern.

The only thing left was to hope that the professor in the Middle Ages could defeat Max and his friends.

Chapter 15

The inside of Castle Dardan was extremely grand. Expensive and exotic antiquities from all around the world were displayed throughout the main areas of the castle, and the castle itself was surrounded by a deep moat. In order to access it, a large drawbridge had to be lowered over the water.

Max, Joe, Arthur, and the Robinsons were being led through a grand corridor. The guards were armed with swords and longbows, so the group knew that an attempt to escape would be very foolish.

"Where are you taking us?" asked Mrs Robinson.

"Keep quiet," responded one of the guards.

"We demand an audience with The Professor," said Max.

"Halt!" shouted the head guard, turning to face Max. "Who do you think you are? The Professor doesn't waste his time with common thieves."

"He's our dad!" shouted Patrick and Lily in unison.

"Your father?!" exclaimed a shocked Arthur. "Why didn't you tell me?"

"Quiet!" shouted the head guard. "Enough with this foolishness."

The guards continued leading the prisoners towards the end of the corridor, at which point they stopped in front of a large stone door. The head guard pulled on a rope that was hanging next to the door. A second later, a bell could be heard ringing in the room beyond.

"You've seen the nicest parts of the castle... now you'll see the worst parts," said the head guard, smirking. "We always bring prisoners this way so they can see amazing wonders they will never be able to have."

The stone door opened, and the prisoners were led down a steep staircase into the basement area of the castle. It was dark, damp, and smelly.

"Welcome to your new home," laughed the head guard as he pushed the prisoners into a small cell. "Enjoy."

"What now?" asked Patrick once the guard had left.

"Don't worry, this is all part of the plan," said Max. "Be patient. I asked you to ask for your dad for a reason. We won't be here long."

"I'm annoyed that you didn't tell me about that," said Arthur, "but I understand why you didn't."

"Wait," said Joe, looking around at the group. "Where's Mo?!"

"He must have got away and hidden somewhere," said Arthur. "Possibly with Monty."

Joe groaned. He didn't like thinking about his friend being out there, all alone, in this strange land.

"If he's with Monty," Arthur said gently, "he'll be fine."

Reluctantly, Joe nodded. It wasn't as if he could do anything about it now. Not from inside this cell, anyway.

Patrick decided that now was the right time to tell the rest of the group that he'd sabotaged Dardan's main console back in 2022.

"So, Dardan can't travel anywhere," he finished. "He's trapped in his cave; he can't risk going outside because of the dinosaurs." He took the portal energiser chip out of his pocket. "I took this during all the chaos in the cave. As long as we have it, the portal to the Middle Ages is the last one that will be opened. Dardan won't be following us here."

"Can't he just make another chip?" asked Lily.

"Impossible," replied Max. "The technology only exists on Proxima Centauri b."

Having listened to this strange conversation and taken everything in, Arthur was more confused than ever. "Are you telling me that you all come from the future?" he asked.

Max decided it was time to tell Arthur the full story, and everyone else agreed.

So, the prisoners passed the time by telling the story of their travels through time and, before long, they heard footsteps approaching. These footsteps stopped directly outside the cell, and moments later they heard the unmistakable sound of a key entering a lock.

"Here we go," proclaimed Max.

***

"What's our plan then?" asked Mo as he looked out at the horde of knights gathered in the alleyway.

"We wait for a signal," replied an exasperated Merlin. "I've just told you that."

Mo moved away from the door and sat down next to Monty on the floor of the main room. "You know, most people think you're a magician or a wizard," he said.

Merlin sighed. "As I told you, there is no such thing as a wizard."

Suddenly, a loud squawking sound came from outside. Instantly, the knights all reached for their longbows, aiming them upwards.

"No one is going to harm those birds," ordered Merlin, walking over to the front door. The knights returned the longbows to the carriers on their backs. "These are not the type of birds you are familiar with."

Mo ran back to the door and looked up. Merlin was right: these birds looked completely different. They had much bigger heads, and they looked far more powerful than the birds he was used to[6].

"What are they?" asked Mo.

"Transport," replied Merlin.

The birds landed in the alleyway. There was precisely one bird for every knight.

"These birds are our friends," announced Merlin. "You will each partner up with one and fly into the sky. It is completely safe."

"Are you sure?" shouted one of the knights, sounding nervous. "They look vicious. Is it really safe?"

"Yes," replied Merlin calmly. "They are my friends."

The nervous knights each sat on a bird and, one by one, they took off. Mo had seen some strange sights over the past few days, but this was definitely the most awesome.

6. These 'birds' are a type of flying dinosaur called a Dimorphodon

156

"Why are they helping us?" asked Mo.

Merlin looked at Mo and winked. "Perhaps I do know some magic."

"I knew it!" laughed Mo. "I've never seen that type of bird before though. Where did they come from?"

"I'm not sure," Merlin admitted. "They only exist in Camelot. I've been training them with food for a while now; I seem to have gained their trust so much that my knights are now able to fly safely with them."

Mo looked up again. The birds and knights were nowhere to be seen.

"They will be waiting for the same signal we are," Merlin told him. "Just relax. We have some time to wait."

Mo sat down in front of the fire, next to the bear. He couldn't pretend he wasn't nervous, but he knew that Monty would protect him. He was also convinced that Merlin was a wizard. How else could he control those birds?

Monty was sleeping and, as Mo was feeling tired now too, he

closed his eyes.

As the fire burned cosily in the corner of the room, he drifted slowly off to sleep.

***

"Come with us!" ordered the guard who was standing at the now open cell door.

The group of friends exited the cell and followed the guard back up the stairs that led to the main part of the castle.

"Remember: don't get too emotional," Max said to the Robinsons. "We need to stick to the plan."

Mrs Robinson and the twins nodded in response, their expressions a mix of nerves and excitement.

After a short walk through the castle, they arrived at a large ornate door.

"Wait," ordered the guard as he knocked on the door.

It didn't take long before the door opened, revealing another guard on the other side. "I'll take them," he said to guard number one.

On the other side of the door there was another steep staircase, and displayed on the walls of this staircase were pictures of Dardan, Verissimus, and the twins' dad. As they approached the top of the staircase, they could hear a familiar voice.

"It's Dad!" exclaimed Lily.

By now the Robinsons were getting extremely nervous. They had heard horrible stories about 'The Professor' from Arthur, including all the terrible things he'd done.

He's being controlled, Patrick kept telling himself. *We can make him better.*

At the top of the stairs, they entered a large room. It was enormous and luxurious with dark windows. In the middle of the room was a large round table.

"Follow me," said the guard.

They walked past the round table and, as they approached the end of the room, they could see a familiar figure. He was looking out

158

of the window, facing in the opposite direction.

"It's Dad!" shouted Patrick as he ran in front of the guard.

"Come back!" ordered the guard.

"It's okay," said the figure at the end of the room, "you may leave us."

"If you insist, sir," the guard replied as he left the room through a side door.

Slowly, the figure at the end of the room started turning around. "It's very good to see you all again. It's been far too long."

Max, Joe, and the Robinsons couldn't believe what they were seeing. The man standing in front of them was indeed the professor, but he was much older than the professor they knew. He was at least 70 years of age.

"This must be very confusing for you," he said, "but it's been 30 years since I last saw you all."

Chapter 16

"W-what?" stuttered Patrick, as Mrs Robinson and Lily burst into tears.

"I don't understand," said Mrs Robinson.

The professor looked at his family and smiled. "Have you already forgotten how confusing time travel can be? I was brought to Camelot 30 years ago. I have been the supreme ruler since then. The portal brought you to the right place, but it was 30 years out."

"We've come to rescue you, Dad," said Lily quietly.

The professor laughed. "Why would I need rescuing?"

Max took a step towards the professor. "Where are Dardan and Verissimus?"

The professor explained that they occasionally visited to check how things were, but that most of the time he was left to rule Camelot alone.

"What are you going to do with us?" asked Mrs Robinson, still shocked at seeing her husband looking 30 years older.

"Nothing," replied the professor. "I'm glad that we're all together again. You will stay here in the castle."

Patrick and Lily exchanged nervous glances. It was good to see their dad again – but not like this.

"How can you understand what people are saying?" asked Max. "The Lingua worm I gave you will have crawled out decades ago."

"Good question," responded the professor. "It was difficult, but I had to learn Latin. It took a couple of years to be fluent. I will teach you all how to speak it once your worms have expired."

"All of us?" asked Joe.

The professor looked directly at Joe. "I'm afraid not. You, Max, and Arthur are not family. You will be executed in the morning." A half-smile appeared on his lips as he stared into the distance. "Oh, I do love a good execution."

As Joe started to panic, four guards appeared from a hidden door.

"Take these three traitors away!" ordered the professor.

"No!" shouted Patrick and Lily in unison.

"Fear not!" shouted Arthur as he pulled out what looked like a wand from one of his shoes. "This is all part of the plan."

Arthur pointed the wand at the guards and they immediately turned to ice. "They'll be okay," Arthur told the rest of the group. "Once the ice defrosts, they'll be absolutely fine again." He then pointed the wand at the professor.

"Dad!" shouted Patrick as he looked at the now completely frozen professor.

"I've known who you all were all along," Arthur explained to the group. "I'm sorry I didn't tell you. I was sent to meet you by Merlin; you were the only way we could get an audience with the professor. Don't worry – we're going to make him better."

Arthur approached the professor and asked Max to join him. "We need to remove the thing that is controlling him."

For a few moments, Max studied the frozen professor. "That's easy," he said, reaching out and removing a bracelet that was on his right wrist. "We need to destroy this."

Before anyone could say anything in response, Patrick ran over to Max, took hold of the bracelet, and threw it to the ground. Lily and Mrs Robinson quickly ran over to the bracelet and began stamping on it for good measure.

"It must be completely destroyed so that the power Dardan had over your dad is removed forever," explained Max.

Within a couple of minutes there was nothing left of the bracelet; the remains had been thrown onto the fire at the end of the room.

"It's time to call for reinforcements," declared Arthur as he held his wand aloft.

***

"Wake up," said Merlin, "it's time."

Mo opened his eyes and looked at Merlin. "I thought this had all been a dream," he said sleepily.

"It's time that we defeat the forces of evil once and for all," said Merlin. "The knights will already be approaching the castle from the air." He paused, staring at Mo for a second. "Can you keep a secret?"

"Yes," replied Mo.

"I am a wizard," admitted Merlin, pulling out a wand from inside his cloak. "Let's go!" he shouted as a flash of light appeared from the tip of the wand. The room started to spin and, within a few seconds, Mo, Merlin, and Monty found themselves in the same room as Max and the others.

"Mo, you're okay!" shouted Joe.

A dizzy and confused Mo didn't answer; he just fell to the floor.

"He'll be okay in a minute or two," said Merlin.

A squawking sound could be heard coming from outside. "Here come the reinforcements," said Arthur.

Joe looked out of a now clear window to see an incredible sight. A whole army of knights were arriving in the castle grounds on what looked like large flying dinosaurs. They certainly had the element of surprise, and the knights quickly took control of the castle. "We're winning!" Joe shrieked as he watched the battle below.

"Good," said Max. "Now, we need to get back to the Cretaceous period. We have to stop Dardan from stealing the pyramids and gaining the power to transport his Troodon army."

"What about my dad?" asked Lily. "He's… old."

"Time travel is complicated," replied Max. "If we are going to put things back to normal then only Joe and I can go back. Everyone who is at time ground zero will stay exactly as they are. That means that Mo will only be able to speak Latin and your dad will stay as a 70-year-old man."

"Will we remember anything at all?" asked Mrs Robinson.

"I'm afraid not," replied Max. "It's the only way."

"It's the only way," a quiet voice repeated from the end of the room.

"Dad!" shouted Lily and Patrick together as they ran over to hug the professor.

"I'm sorry for everything I've done," said the professor, tears filling his eyes as he hugged his children. "I don't want to remember any of the terrible things I've been involved in. This is the only way."

Mrs Robinson and the twins nodded sadly.

"You'll need to get back to Dardan's cave," continued the professor. "I'll arrange for this to happen immediately." He looked at Arthur. "You are the rightful ruler of Camelot. This will also be announced immediately."

"I'm sorry," said Arthur, "but you will need to be imprisoned for all the evil things you've done. I know it wasn't your fault, but you won't be safe in Camelot if I let you leave."

The professor nodded. "I agree," he said quietly before looking at Max and Joe. "You'll need this." He went over to a drawer and pulled out a trekker. "This will get you back to the cave."

"Thank you," said Joe, getting a little emotional.

"Yes," said Max, "this trekker will be very useful indeed."

Max and Joe said their final goodbyes, and then it was the turn of the Robinsons.

"We'll never see you again," said Mrs Robinson with tears in her eyes.

Lily and Patrick each gave Max and Joe a hug as they said goodbye.

Finally, Mo approached Joe. "I hope you can fix this, otherwise I'll be stuck here forever. Hopefully I'll see you at school soon."

"You will," said Joe, smiling, "but you won't believe any of this happened!"

"It's been a pleasure," said King Arthur, holding out his hand and shaking everyone else's in turn. "Good luck."

"Let's go!" said Max as he held the trekker out in front of him. Within seconds, the image of Dardan's cave had appeared in the glass.

***

The cave was just as deserted as when they'd left it. The console still didn't have any blinking lights on its dashboard.

"How are we going to get this thing working?" asked Joe.

"With this," replied Max as he pulled the portal energiser chip out of his pocket. "Remember that Patrick took it from the console in 2022. It's risky, though," he added, "because when I put this back it will also be in the 2022 console." He leaned over, studying the dashboard. "The chip that's already here needs repairing. This is much easier."

Joe suddenly remembered something. "Before you do that, we need to leave the trekker in the pit."

"Of course – good thinking," agreed Max.

After they'd left the trekker in the pit, they headed back to the console. Max removed the faulty energiser chip and replaced it with the one from 2022.

"Here we go again," said Max as the cave started to shake. The portal appeared in front of them and, cautiously, they walked through.

Part 6: Back to the Cretaceous

Chapter 17

Max and Joe found themselves standing at the foot of the volcano, just outside the entrance of the cave.

"Dardan will not be expecting us," said Max. "We are here a year earlier than last time, and he's only been here a few weeks. We should be able to surprise him."

"How exactly are we going to do that?" asked Joe.

"We are going to use the technology here to contact my planet," Max explained. "As you already know, Dardan is an escaped prisoner."

Joe nodded.

"Come on – let's head in."

Together, they cautiously entered the volcano and headed towards the central cavern.

Once again, the cavern appeared to be deserted. Dardan was nowhere to be seen.

"Where do you think he is?" asked Joe.

"He'll be around here somewhere," replied Max. "Quick – let's get to work."

Max and Joe approached the console, which was livelier than Joe had ever seen it before, with lots of blinking lights.

"It looks brand new!" exclaimed Joe.

"It is," replied Max as he started pressing buttons on the console, "and even now the Chicxulub impactor is enough to power the console."

Joe noticed a small green light flashing on the monitor. "What's that?" he asked.

Before Max could answer, however, they heard a loud howl coming from behind them.

"Maxelon?" asked a surprised Dardan.

"Hello Dardan," replied Max, turning to face the Wolfian. "It's good to see you."

Dardan stared at him in shock. He couldn't understand how Max had found him; he hadn't done anything to give away his position.

"It looks like you've only just arrived here," said Max. "This console is newly grown. Where's the escape pod you were in?"

"It was destroyed when I crashed here. Luckily, I had a small supply of *Organa-tech* seeds, as I imagine you did as well."

"Yes, I did," replied Max. "I crashed much further into the future. I was found by my friend Joe here."

"Hi," said Joe, not knowing what else to say.

Max looked angrily at Dardan. "You've done a lot of damage to this planet. We are here to stop you."

Dardan frowned in confusion. "I haven't done anything yet. Ah… so that means you must have come from my future?"

Max nodded. "And now it's time to go home."

The green light on the monitor started getting brighter and brighter. Then, suddenly, a beam of light shot out from the monitor and shone directly onto Dardan. He was unable to move.

"We'll leave him here for a while. In the meantime, we have a short errand to carry out," said Max.

By now Joe was feeling very confused. *What's going on*? he thought.

Max approached the console again and pressed some more buttons. Soon, there was the familiar shaking of a portal opening. "We need to go nine months into the future," he explained. "There are some people we need to rescue."

The Robinsons, thought Joe. *Of course*!

They stepped into the portal and, once again, found themselves right outside the volcano. The portal was still open.

"We are using the power from my planet," Max explained to

Joe. "That's where the green ray of light has come from. This portal will stay open for as long as we need it to. It's only programmed for us and the Robinsons, so nothing else will be able to cross through it."

The two friends started walking and, before long, they had made their way back to the Robinsons' treehouse.

They approached the stilted house and shouted up to the Robinsons.

Professor Robinson appeared moments later, looking down at the ground in shock. "There are two people here… and they seem to know who we are!" he said to his family.

Patrick, Lily, and Mrs Robinson quickly joined the professor.

"Can we come up?" shouted Max.

Rather reluctantly, the professor lowered the ladder as he tried to reassure his family. "There are only two of them. It will be fine."

Max and Joe climbed to the top of the ladder and entered the treehouse.

"You're young again," Joe said to a very confused professor.

"Sorry, what?"

Smiling, Joe explained how they'd come to rescue them before the meteor that causes the extinction of the dinosaurs hit Earth.

The Robinsons were very confused but extremely grateful, especially when they realised they would finally be able to go home. For some reason, they trusted these two strangers – it was as if, on some level, they felt like they knew them.

So, after a quick family meeting, the Robinsons packed their essentials and headed into the jungle.

Before long, they were all back at the portal. They crossed through and returned to the central cavern, where Dardan was still trapped in the green light.

***

"This will take you back to the exact time in the future that you left," Max explained as he opened another portal. "It will be as if you never left." He paused for a moment, before addressing the professor directly. "Please don't mess around with time travel again."

"It was an accident," explained the professor, "but I'll be destroying all my inventions when we get back home."

Mrs Robinson nodded emphatically. "We certainly will. And thank you both again, so much."

After saying their goodbyes, the Robinson family walked into the portal and disappeared.

"Why didn't we rescue them from an earlier time?" asked Joe. "I mean… they didn't need to be stuck here for so long, did they?"

"We already knew that they were safe," Max explained. "I needed to make sure they were here long enough to put the professor off attempting time travel again."

Before Joe could respond, the cave started to shake.

"We need to destroy this console," said Max.

Joe looked at him in horror. "But then how do we get back to 2022?" he asked.

"We don't," said Max as the console started to spark. "We are going somewhere else."

The green light that continued to cover Dardan had now started to illuminate the whole cave.

Suddenly, Dardan disappeared.

Joe looked around, panicked. "Max, what's happening?"

There was no answer. Max had also disappeared.

Joe looked down at his hand and, to his horror, it seemed to be disintegrating. He could see the cells in his body separating and then, suddenly, he was no longer in the cave.

He looked out at the landscape around him. He was surrounded by green mountains and the sky was tinged with green. It was like seeing the Northern Lights, but they were everywhere.

"Are you okay?"

Joe turned around to see Max standing behind him. "What happened?" he asked, his gaze moving from Max to their strange yet beautiful surroundings. Dardan – who was still bathed in the strange green light – was standing nearby, a blank expression on his face.

"The cave was destroyed. Earth is back to normal. There has never been an Order of Verissimus. We did it."

"Where are we?" asked Joe.

"Home," replied Max.

Part 7: Proxima Centauri b

Chapter 18

The temperature on the planet was very similar to England in the spring, and the mountains looked just like the mountains Joe was used to, but other than that... it was all so surreal.

Joe couldn't believe what he was seeing. This was the strangest experience of all the strange experiences he'd had recently.

"How will I get back to Earth?" he asked.

"Don't worry. I'll get you home as soon as the authorities have collected Dardan," replied Max, "which should be very soon."

"Why didn't you send me home after the Robinsons had gone?" asked Joe. "I don't understand why I'm here."

"It was too risky to open another portal when the gateway to this planet had been opened," Max told him. "The console was very unstable. I didn't want you to get stranded in a strange time."

In the distance, Joe could hear a futuristic swishing noise. It seemed to be getting closer and closer.

Dardan looked towards the approaching vehicle, smiled, and then started to howl.

"Why is he so happy?" asked Joe.

Max looked up and saw the vehicle that was approaching. "Run!" he shouted. "It's the Wolfians!"

"Who?" screamed Joe.

Max grabbed hold of Joe's hand and, together, they ran into a nearby cave.

"What's going on?" shouted Joe. "I thought Dardan was being captured by the authorities!"

Max shook his head. "He was. I'm not sure how his friends knew he was here."

Outside the cave, the Wolfian spaceship had now landed and released Dardan from the green light. Within seconds he had escaped with the other Wolfians.

Max and Joe left the cave just in time to see the Wolfian spaceship accelerate away.

"Maxelon?"

Max turned around to see one of his best friends. "Jaxelon!" he said. "It's so good to see you. This is my friend, Joe. He's from Earth."

Jaxelon – along with a large group of Tamirans – approached

Joe. "It's very nice to meet you," said Jaxelon, "now let's get back to Tamiran."

***

Tamiran was beautiful. It was a partially submerged domed island city floating in the middle of an enormous ocean. Joe and Max were travelling on a monorail system, which was giving Joe an amazing tour of the city.

"The Wolfians can't enter the dome; they are terrified of water," Max explained. "They will not cross the ocean, but ⌐ just in case – our army is guarding every entrance. You don't have to worry – this dome has kept us safe for centuries."

"Why did Dardan want to take over Earth if he's scared of water?" asked Joe. "Earth is 71% water."

"Yes, it is," agreed Max, "but that means 29% is dry, and if it's enough for humans, it's enough for Dardan and the Wolfians as well."

The monorail stopped outside a large, modern-looking building made almost entirely of green crystals. Joe gawped at it in awe.

"Let's go in," said Max.

"Where are we now?" asked Joe as they entered the strange structure. It looked like a type of laboratory, which made Joe nervous.

"There's nothing to worry about," said Max. "The Lingua worm inside your ear will be ready to crawl out soon. We're just going to remove it – and give you a gift."

"A gift?" repeated Joe.

"Yes," said Max. "We are going to make a small adjustment to your brain."

"What?!" shouted Joe.

"Don't worry. It will give you the permanent ability to understand and speak any language in the universe."

Joe considered this for a moment – he certainly liked the sound of it. "That will definitely help me pass French and Spanish," he said to Max. "It doesn't involve a worm, does it?"

"No," replied Max as he exited the main lab, leaving Joe alone. He could see Joe through a large window in the next room – a room that was filled with dashboards and buttons – and he could talk to Joe through a speaker attached to the wall. "No worms at all. We'll get started right away. Just sit in that chair over there."

Joe did as he was told, ready but nervous for the procedure to start.

Fortunately, the whole thing was quick and painless. The lab was illuminated with a very fast flashing green light and, before long, Joe found that he was fluent in every language in the universe.

"This is going to be amazing!" Joe said excitably as Max returned to the lab and sat down.

"We need to go to Wolfian and catch Dardan," Max said, getting back to business. "If we don't, he'll make his way back to Earth, and – this time – he might not go alone." He shook his head. "Just think about how much damage he did on his own. Now imagine a whole platoon of Wolfian soldiers."

Joe gulped. "How are we going to catch him?"

"We can talk about that later. The first thing we need to find out is how the Wolfians knew that Dardan was being brought back to this planet. Come on, let's go – we've got a meeting to attend."

Max and Joe left the lab and headed for the central parliament building. They found their way to the presidential room and took their seats in the VIP section.

The government had called an urgent meeting, Max explained to Joe that all the most important and powerful Tamirans were going to be in attendance. Joe found it extremely surreal to be sitting amongst all the VIPs of Tamiran, but rather than being scared or overwhelmed, he actually felt pretty excited.

The room was incredibly noisy, with lots of excited and angry chatter taking place. Joe was trying his best to listen to what was being said when, suddenly, the chatter stopped and everyone turned to face the front of the room.

"That's the president," whispered Max.

The man standing on the stage cut an imposing figure. He was at least six feet tall with a bushy black beard, and he was wearing a black robe and wig.

He looks like a judge, thought Joe.

Moments later, the president started to speak. He thanked everyone for attending this important meeting, and he expressed how extremely pleased he was to hear that Maxelon had returned safely. He also welcomed Joe to Tamiran and said that he would always be welcome here.

Then, the president's upbeat mood vanished and, suddenly, everything became very sombre indeed.

"We have discovered that we have a traitor in this room," he said, causing all the Tamirans in the crowd to gasp in shock.

Everything went dark, and a green ray of light began moving around the room.

"What's going on?" whispered Joe as the light moved directly in front of his face.

"The light reads brainwaves," Max explained. "It will shine directly onto the traitor."

The ray of light continued to spin around the room for at least a minute before it suddenly stopped.

"No!" cried Max.

The light was shining directly onto Jaxelon.

The presidential guards quickly apprehended Jaxelon and took him to the front of the room.

"Explain yourself!" shouted the president.

Jaxelon smirked. "You people are pathetic," he said. "Surely, you don't think I did this alone, did you? The Wolfians have promised us riches beyond our wildest dreams when we go to Earth."

"Us?" asked the president.

Suddenly, the door to the room burst open and 30 armed Tamirans ran into the room.

As the panic began to escalate, it became clear that there was much worse to come. From outside the room, a chilling sound echoed around the Tamiran streets.

It was the sound of a hundred howling Wolfians.

***

The panic and confusion sweeping through the presidential room was overwhelming. It wasn't clear who was good or bad, and the terrifying sound of the approaching Wolfians was getting louder and louder.

"What do we do?" asked a panic-stricken Joe.

Max didn't know how to answer. He didn't have any ideas and he wasn't even sure who they could trust anymore.

Moments later, the Wolfians entered the room and ordered everyone – including the president – to gather in the centre of the room. The treacherous Tamirans stood at the perimeter to stop anyone leaving. They were pointing their guns at the prisoners, who were forced to face the stage as a now familiar face came into view.

"Welcome friends and prisoners!" he announced. "It's very good of you all to join us here today. You are being very welcoming to us on our first visit to Tamiran."

Joe was frantically looking around the room to find a way to

179

escape. He was getting well and truly fed up with Dardan.

Dardan continued his speech. "We need you to share your technology with us, as we are planning to leave this planet and go to Earth. You WILL help us get there," he demanded. "We are grateful to the Tamirans who have already made the right decision to join us. You will all be rewarded when we get to Earth."

Max was beginning to understand how Dardan and the Wolfians had managed to get to Tamiran: the traitors (including his friend Jaxelon) must have used a trekker. They hadn't needed to cross the water at all.

Joe was pondering how they could get out of this and permanently defeat Dardan, and then he remembered what Max had said about the Wolfians and their fear of water. Glancing at the windows in the corners of the room, he realised something very interesting – this room was underwater.

"We demand that you provide us with your entire supply of *Organa-tech* seeds so that we can grow your technology on Earth," continued Dardan. "I have already tested it there and, from what I hear from Maxelon, it worked amazingly well. It's a shame he had to mess things up, but never mind. We'll try again."

Joe had also noticed that one of the traitors had accidently – and without noticing – dropped his gun on the floor. *How sloppy,* he thought as he headed in the direction of the misplaced weapon.

Everyone in the room was so completely focused on Dardan that they failed to notice Joe carefully making his way over to the gun. He picked it up and, very carefully, examined it.

By now, Max had noticed what Joe was doing.

The gun had only one button on it. *This looks straightforward,* thought Joe, pointing the gun at one of the windows and pushing the button.

Everyone in the room could now see what Joe was doing as a green ray of light shot out the end of the gun and hit the window.

"Stop him!" shouted Dardan.

It was too late.

The window started to crack before breaking completely and letting in gallons and gallons of water from outside. As the room

"We surrender!" they all shouted, giving the Tamiran army (who were very competent swimmers) the opportunity to capture both the Wolfians and the traitors. Joe smiled as he watched the army do their job.

Within a few seconds, the window had started to seal itself and the water was already being pumped out of the room.

"It's a self-fixing window," said Max. "*Organa-tech*. Well done. That was an excellent idea, Joe – you've saved Tamiran!"

Joe's smile turned into an excited grin.

Dardan had also been taken into custody and, once he was gone from the room, the president returned to the stage.

"We owe our Earth friend our gratitude," he announced. "His smart thinking has prevented a terrible tragedy. Joe, please join me on stage."

"Go ahead," Max said to his friend.

Feeling excited, but also a little nervous at being the centre of attention, Joe made his way to the stage to rapturous applause.

The president placed a green medal around his neck. "You will always be welcome on Tamiran. What can we do to thank you?"

Joe thought about this for a few seconds. "I would like to go home, please."

"Of course," said the president.

***

Dardan, the Wolfians, and the Tamiran traitors were tried and convicted the following morning – which was made easy as they all pleaded guilty. They were imprisoned in an underwater prison dome.

"It's impossible to escape," Max explained to Joe, as they both stood at the entrance to the Space Sling.

"Good," said Joe. He'd had enough of Dardan for one lifetime – or several of them.

"This is the quickest and most efficient way to get you home," Max explained, gesturing to the Space Sling. "It will send you back to the exact time just after you entered my cave. You won't fall into the hole so you won't enter the cave. Go straight home. Your future will be completely unwritten."

"Will I remember all of this?" asked Joe. The thought of forgetting it all seemed so unfair.

"I have a feeling you'll remember," said Max, smiling.

Joe was starting to get upset. "I'm going to miss you," he said quietly.

Max nodded. "I'm going to miss you too, but I'm sure we'll see each other again."

After saying his final goodbye, Joe entered the Space Sling and strapped himself in. It looked like one of those rides at the fair that catapult people into the air.

Joe felt terrified, but he was ready to get back to his normal life. This had been the weirdest, scariest, and most amazing few weeks of his life – but now he needed to go home.

A countdown began. "Five… four… three… two… one!"

The Space Sling shot into the air and Joe started to feel dizzy. He could see flashing lights right in front of him, which got faster and faster… until it all went dark.

Part 8: Home

Chapter 19

Sunday 9th January 2022

Joe opened his eyes.

"Are you okay, young man?" shouted a man in a hi-visibility jacket. "You almost got caught in an explosion! We had to destroy an unexploded bomb from World War II."

"Yes, I'm fine," said Joe as he got up, dusted himself off, and ran home.

Mrs Jackson and Eve were drinking coffee in the living room when, suddenly, Joe burst through the front door.

"Calm down!" exclaimed Mrs Jackson. "What's the rush? What on Earth are you wearing?"

Joe ran over to his mum and gave her an enormous hug. "I love you so much," he said.

Mrs Jackson hugged him back, surprised and overwhelmed by this unexpected display of emotion. "What's all this about?" she asked.

"I just love you," replied Joe.

"What a lovely young man you are," said Eve. "Patricia, you are a very lucky lady."

Joe pulled back from the hug, smiling at his mum, before leaving the living room and running upstairs.

In his bedroom, he immediately logged onto his computer and – much to his relief – was able to log onto the internet. He checked the location of the pyramids. They were in Egypt. He checked the location of Stonehenge. It was near Salisbury. He checked for the existence of 'birds'. Thankfully, there were plenty of regular, normal birds – and no pterodactyls.

Thank you, Max, he thought as he looked at the medal he was still wearing around his neck.

Next, Joe checked his social media accounts. They were back. He checked Mo's page. It was exactly how he remembered Mo's page looking before the time travel adventure began.

What about the Robinsons? he thought. After a quick search he found the pages for both Lily and Patrick and requested a friendship connection. *I can't wait to see them all again.*

After his internet session, Joe lay down on his bed and called for Milo, who came scampering into the room.

"I've missed you so much," he said to the cat before looking over at his window and out at the early evening winter sky. "I've been on the most amazing adventure!"

The End